"From the Face of the Earth..."

by Ruth D. Hein

Ruth D. Hein (signature)

Daily Globe
Worthington, Minnesota

1998

"From the Face of the Earth..."
Copyright 1998
Ruth D. Hein
Worthington, MN 56187

Published by Daily Globe, Worthington, Minnesota

Other books by author:
Ghostly Tales of Minnesota, 1992
Ghostly Tales of Iowa, 1996 (coauthored with Vicky L. Hinsenbrock)
Eggplant Sandwiches/ A Book of [My] Poems, 1989
Ghostly Tales of Southwest Minnesota, 1989, out of print
Ghostly Tales of the Black Hills and Badlands, 1999, pending

Cover photos by Brian Korthals
Project coordinator, Cindy Conway, The Printers
Other photos, Ruth D. Hein unless otherwise noted

First printing August 1998

ISBN 0-9625304-1-7

This book is dedicated to...

pioneering families like the Olesons and many others who established homes and settlements in the Midwest in the mid-to-later 1800s and then moved on to other new beginnings, making the way smoother for those of us who followed.

Acknowledgments...

I wish to extend my sincere thanks to all who had anything to do with making this fictionalized history possible, including the pioneers and others of the time and place who are the characters in the story.

Thanks are also due to members of the Fury and Langer families, Jerry Braun, Lew Hudson, Ray Crippen, and others for their historical input, and to my friends and relatives who read it at various stages and offered helpful suggestions. They, along with the publisher and others, helped to make it the best book possible.

I also wish to sincerely thank W.Donald and Glenda Olsen, with whose help I was able to use some Norwegian words and phrases that would still come naturally and easily to the story's Oleson family, before the English words, at least for their first few years of living away from their native land and language.

Thanks also to Tim and Mick for helping me learn to use my new computer and to keyboard the entire book on it and save it to a diskette.

Introduction
by Historian Lew Hudson

In this book, Ruth Hein walks down an historical trail I followed for many years as an historian, reporter and feature writer for the Worthington Daily Globe.

The lost colony reported first by Historian Arthur P. Rose in his History of Nobles County (1908) has long intrigued me. I spent countless hours searching for them. Every lead terminated in a blind alley.

Where did they go? Why did none return? Why are there no letters? Didn't they even come back to visit? Weren't they curious about how the country was eventually settled?

The most promising lead started and ended in the cemetery at Ellsworth where there is a grave of a Betsey Oleson whose date of birth is close to that of one of the characters in Hein's story, but I could never learn a thing about her.

I can, however, speak to the accuracy of Hein's description of the island homestead. I was secretary of the Nobles County Park Commission when the 10-acre island was bought by the county in 1965 and made into the beautiful park it is today.

I was present that summer when the Minnesota State Archaeologist, the late Dr. Elden Johnson, made a preliminary survey and turned up a prehistoric fire pit on the southwest end of the island. That led to a 1965 excavation by U of M archaeologists Charles Watrall and Terry Booth which turned up artifacts attesting to Indian usage as far back as the time of Christ.

Hein's contention the area was loved and used extensively by Indians is further borne out by a 1973-75 archaeological excavation of a burial mound atop a small hill a quarter mile west of the island by the Sioux Archaeological Society headed by myself and Wes Bakker of Westbrook.

That project turned up the remains of at least 15 human beings accompanied by numerous artifacts dating to the time period 700 to 900 A.D. A report of that project is filed in local libraries and with the Minnesota Archaeological Society.

About 1970, the Sioux Archaeological Society conducted an excavation of the cabin site in the center of the island.

While it was known to have been the home of the Benjamin Tanner family from 1867 until about 1871, the cabin was built over a dugout that probably dated to the time of the lost colony. In her book, Hein attributes the dugout to the Olesons. She may well be right.

In any case, there is no record of anyone living on the island after 1871.

The Tanner cabin excavation produced hundreds of artifacts dating to the mid years of the 19th century including the china doll with the broken leg which plays a part in Hein's story. The doll and hundreds of artifacts along with a full report of the excavation is in the hands of the park commission and available for review by interested persons.

In telling her story, Hein blends historic fact and informed guesses to dramatize the challenges and rewards of life on the untamed prairie. With luck, her book might be the key that finally unlocks the mystery of those 35 stalwart men, women and children who blazed the trail the rest of us followed to Nobles County.

If not, it's still a good yarn.

The Bicentennial Tree near Fury's Island.

Preface

A historical mystery had its beginnings in the northeast corner of Nobles County in southwest Minnesota in the early 1860s. It is still a mystery even after well over a hundred years have passed.

As the frontier pushed on westward with the many immigrants of the early 1800s, the land that is now the State of Minnesota was still a territory, but by 1850 there were about 6,000 white people living in it.

Then in 1853 a man named William LeDuc set up a fine exhibit at the world's fair held at the Crystal Palace in New York. To show the superior grains that could be grown in the fertile soil of Minnesota Territory, he gathered wheat, rye, oats, barley and corn. He also displayed furs from the trading post at Mendota, samples of wild rice, and an Indian canoe. His display attracted the attention of many immigrants and others thinking of coming to America at that time.

Many farmers left their homelands in Europe to look for land in southern Minnesota. Others who had already settled in the eastern and northern United States moved on west by the time the territory became a state in May, 1858.

By 1855 about 54,000 whites, many of them farmers, were living in Minnesota Territory. The whites were so eager to expand into new territory that they went west and became "squatters" on land even before the government surveys and land offices were established and before the Indians were removed. As soon as the land was opened for settlement the whites wanted to take over on it even though conditions were not yet right for occupation by whites. And since the spirit of many pioneers included an urge to move on to new horizons and a driving desire to occupy land uncrowded and undeveloped, they continued to move on. Southwest Minnesota was beginning to fill up fast.

As more people came and the small settlements grew, stores, hotels and mills appeared on the horizon.

Although the settlement of 1856 at Springfield had been attacked on March 26, 1857, white people were gradually moving into the area again soon afterward. Jackson County was designated in May 1857 with Springfield, renamed Jackson, as the county seat. There was a settlement at Lake Shetek to the north in 1857. Mankato was the next town to the east, and farther east at New Ulm a group of Germans had started their town in 1855.

Farther south, in western Iowa, there were well-established towns like Fort Dodge and Webster City, but that was understandable because Iowa had become a state in 1846, twelve years before Minnesota Territory had become a state on May 24, 1858. And so far, most of the Minnesota settlements were in the eastern part of the new state.

The people at Spirit Lake and Lake Okoboji and Springfield had had a hard time of it. Most of them were killed, some brutally. A few were taken captive.

In 1857, the year before Minnesota Territory became the state, the counties of southwest Minnesota were created and designated. Although in Jackson County and others to the east there were more settlements by 1860, not many had ventured into Nobles and other counties to the north and west.

The author believes that since settlements had been made within the five years previous to 1860 at Spirit Lake, Lake Shetek, and Jackson, there could also have been other small groups of courageous pioneers who ventured into parts of nearby counties in the late 1850s and, when they found a pleasing site, settled there.

There were rumors that the railroad would soon continue west beyond the Mississippi River and through the southern part of the state. Towns were already organized in eastern Minnesota, but some pioneers preferred to go where no town was even organized. They wanted to make a new beginning in every sense of the word.

The Graham Lakes and the land around them presented a pleasing appearance with the two lakes surrounded by fertile soil, much of it wooded. There would be water, wood, and fish and wild game available.

What is the mystery of Graham Lakes? It lies in the question: What happened to the 35 people living in the northeast part of Nobles County near the two lakes after the 1860 federal census listed them?

There was no town at Graham Lakes. Jackson was their postoffice address. Although Jackson had no official postoffice or postmaster until the late 1860s, the proprietor of the general store or his wife would probably have seen to the mail that came in sporadically from Mankato.

The census information was recorded on July 16, 1860 by Elias D. Bruner, assistant marshal, on a page at the end of the Jackson County census.

Eleven homes in Nobles County were visited by Marshal Bruner. Four of the heads of households had personal property listed as a dollar value, but no real estate. All were free and white. None had attended school or married within the year, and only one over twenty could not read or write. None were paupers, deaf and dumb, blind, idiotic or convicts, in the language of the census.

On microfilmed copy of that census as well as on page 41 of Arthur P. Rose's Illustrated History of Nobles County Minnesota (1908), those 35 citizens are listed by name, age, birthplace, and occupation of heads of families. The page in the census is signed by Bruner and dated July 16, 1860 on the microfilmed copy.

A little over two years later, in August of 1862, the Sioux Uprising (also now called the Dakota War, the Minnesota Indian War or the U.S.- Dakota Conflict) resulted in almost complete evacuation of the entire area affected and the abandonment of homes and settlements. No one contacted by the author so far seems to know for sure where these 35 squatters went.

Speculation suggests several possibilities. They may have withdrawn to more heavily settled parts farther east in Minnesota. They could have gone south into northwest Iowa, since five years had passed since the 1857 Spirit Lake Massacre. It is doubtful that they pioneered farther west than the frontier border of the time, which would put them into Indian territory. Monuments at New Ulm and other towns do not include the names of any of these 35, nor have their names been found on written records and reports of the Uprising or on tombstones in the area. Several historical societies and cemetery associations have been contacted.

Several historians have tried to solve the mystery. They are intrigued by the story of those white settlers who seemed to disappear from the face of the earth some time after July 16, 1860. If they had heard of the earlier Spirit Lake Massacre, which is possible, had they also heard a rumor of further action planned for the near future by the restless, angry, starving Indians?

Perhaps the Graham Lakes settlers decided to leave while they could, and escaped the death or captivity that many others suffered. Perhaps they separated and scattered to several different areas beyond the country the Indians moved through.

It is also possible that the next white settlers who came

to the Graham Lakes country in 1867 and 1868 and filed claims on that same land found remnants that would hint of earlier settlement: a pile of rocks here, four flat boulders there, a few logs in another place. They may have found a dugout overgrown with prairie grasses and young trees, or a depression in the ground where a dugout had once been. There may have been ruins of a log and sod shanty or stumps of trees cut down approximately six, seven, and eight years earlier. If there had been log cabins, most of the logs would have disappeared by then, to be used by the Indians or traders and trappers who needed temporary protection from the weather.

The settlers who filed claims and stayed may have correctly assumed that these remnants of earlier occupation of the land were left by trappers and traders. Breaking prairie to transform it to farmland was a difficult, time-consuming process. Many pioneers had to trap and hunt or grow garden produce to survive. All their efforts required hard work. Whether threatened by Indians or discouraged by hard work, hard winters, sickness or loneliness, they may have left remnants of their attempt to tame the prairie or to brave all the hardships.

Land offices would not have recorded the sites these early settlers chose, as they were squatters. They couldn't file claims because the township and section lines were not yet run; the county was not yet divided into townships. And they couldn't have been claim jumpers for that same reason.

Research turned up only two names that matched or came close to those of any of this group. A John Oleson was a private in the Lake Prairie Rangers in the Civil War, in Captain Stone Oleson's Company of Prairie Rangers organized in Nicollet County during the Indian War of 1862. John Oleson, a farmer, was 34 at the time of the 1860 census and lived in the Graham Lakes settlement. In 1862 he would have been 36.

The Lake Prairie Rangers were of the First Sub-District, First Battalion Special Volunteers, State Militia. However, research done by experts at the National Archhives in Washington, DC established that this John Oleson was not the one at Graham Lakes in 1860.

Could the Hans Hanson in the same list of Lake Prairie Rangers be the Henry Hanson, 42, trader, who according to the 1860 federal census came to Graham Lakes country from Tennessee? Again, research at the National Archives established that he was not the same Hanson.

The island on which the Oleson family in this story lived in a dugout and, later, in their cabin is now called Fury's Island, named for Cyril J. and Marie Fury who own part of the land surrounding the lakes. Some of that land has been changed from private farmland into two beautiful county parks used for camping, picnicing, swimming and ice fishing, with boat access to the lakes for fishing and waterskiing.

The lakes have for many years been referred to as East Graham Lake and West Graham Lake. They were named that already in 1838 when Joseph Nicollet and John Fremont and others made an official exploration expedition through the region. They mapped and named many features of the land, including other lakes and creeks in southwest Minnesota. The smaller lake near them is called Jack Lake. The slough is nearby. Access to the island is still by that narrow neck of land, but not across a farm as it formerly was. Roads have been made for easier access so that more people can enjoy the beauty of the lakes and parks.

Researching the history of this early group of Nobles County settlers is extremely absorbing to anyone interested in how life was for the people who were here before us.

Perhaps someone will have information to explain the mystery of what really happened to those first 35 white settlers of Nobles County. Perhaps someone, somewhere, will read this story and recognize in it an ancestor. That would be a wonderful thing to have happen. Otherwise, it will remain a mystery — the mystery of Graham Lakes country in northeastern Nobles County, Minnesota. The mystery of the 35 early settlers, squatters, who were accounted for, but seem to have disappeared from the face of the earth. The mystery of the lost settlement.

Contents

Maria Remembers the Journey Across Minnesota

Maria woke to a shaft of sunlight piercing the darkness in the dugout. With her bright blue eyes she followed the line of light to the opening that served as the doorway. One of the pieces of patchwork quilt had not fallen straight. She could see that it was caught on the wooden handle of the breaking plow standing ready just outside.

Wishing the plow didn't have to be used, but remembering how Papa said, "That doesn't make sense," Maria turned back to see that Papa and Mama were already up and out of the dugout. Then she remembered that Papa was gone yesterday and the day before that, too. But at the moment she felt no loneliness, with her brother George and her little sister Betsy still asleep on the same feathertick that was her own bed.

As she lay there, Maria, the oldest of the three Oleson children, remembered those endless days of traveling in the covered wagon. It seemed to her that they were forever riding toward the sunset. But at least, she thought, the fjaer-dyne — which she would have called it before she learned to speak English — the feathertick made it better. It softened the hardness of the side boards as they leaned against them for so many hours along the way. And she remembered how glad she was to get out and stretch her legs and run, and not ride in the wagon for so long, ever again, when they arrived at the Graham Lakes in the middle of July. The year was 1858.

Moving her right arm lazily and very gently so as not to waken Betsy, Maria reached toward the streak of sunlight. She wanted so much to catch it, to hold it forever, there in the room. For it was just that — one room, not very big — ikke stor, her mother would say.

When they first arrived, Papa had dug into the highest ground on the south side of the island to make it. When he had enough of the dirt bank dug away, he stacked big blocks of root-bound soil on top of each other to complete the side walls. A sandy bank bordered the lake below, out in front of the dugout. Inside the dugout, only a little light came in from above, from between the bundles of slough grass and chunks of sod laid there on slender tree branches to make the roof. But light or not, it was their hjem, their home, their shelter from the weather, and it would "make do," or "klare seg," as Mama often said, until there was time to build a cabin.

Here, at least, there were trees. Most of the land they had seen after crossing the big river was prairie, with no trees for shade or for firewood or for building, except at the edge of the Big Woods.

Maria remembered the Big Woods. They had come upon them sometime after crossing the big river and after Papa bought the oxen and wagon. Except where there were wet areas, and until they arrived at the bend of the Minnesota River at Mankato, the forest stretched along much of the way. The trees were still in full leaf, so the shelter they provided was inviting. The different kinds of oaks and maples with their varied browns and greens against the evergreens made the woods so pleasant when they were there that Maria hoped they could stay.

At first Papa, too, thought he had found a good place to settle. But much of the land there was already taken, so Papa said, "Vi skal ga videre," and they did move on. And now, even that seemed long ago as Maria thought about it again.

Finding the feather-light flecks in the sunlight hard to catch, Maria moved a little too much. Betsy woke up. As she rolled over to get up from the feathertick, a long strand of dry grass came loose from one of the blocks of sod that made the side walls of the dugout. It stuck in her hair and tickled her face and neck when she sat up.

George woke up next. Knowing that there would be no more day dreaming this morning, Maria got up from the soft bed. Dutifully following four-year-old Betsy to the doorway, Maria threw the free end of the quilt aside and stepped out into the sunshine with her sister. Betsy was trying to pull the dry grass out of her unruly curls.

Papa Is Gone to Jackson

Barbara Oleson was coming up the path from the lake, where she had just filled two pails with water. Setting them down, she greeted her daughters lovingly with one wide hug. Betsy, still blinking at the bright daylight, clung to her mother until she picked her up even as she greeted her and asked, "Og hvor er George? Is he still asleep?"

"He's up, Mama. Look — here he comes now," Betsy said as she wriggled all the way down out of her very tall mother's arms.

"I wonder where he thinks he will go exploring today," Maria thought out loud as they all three walked toward George.

The calm expression the children usually saw suddenly became guarded as Barbara said, "Oh, but he must not go alone, Maria." Then, rather than frighten the girls with her real reason, she quickly added, "He does not yet know how to swim. There has not been time for him to learn, since we came..."

"I know, Mama," Maria interrupted. "I will watch out for him."

"And Papa is not home from Jackson yet, or he would need George to help him with the work. Be sure you do keep an eye on him, Maria, and keep him right here on the island."

"I will, Mama," Maria promised. "And I'll play with Betsy, too, out here in the warm sunshine."

Nearer the dugout, George, his light brown hair still tousled from his sleep, greeted them abruptly with a question. "Mama, when will Papa be home?"

"The weather has been good, so it will not be much longer."

George insisted, "But when, Mama? Today?"

"He left the day before yesterday, so he may already be..."

Betsy asked, "Mama, what will Papa bring me?"

George answered before his mother had a chance. "I can tell you that, little sister."

"Well, tell me. What will he bring me?"

George said, "He will bring things Mama needs to cook with, like rice and dried beans."

"Yes, and more salt and flour and sugar," Mama added. "And potatoes. We will need more potatoes very soon."

As much as Barbara wished they could, it wasn't possible to send Papa to Jackson often. For one thing, it used up about three days of good field work time. For another, it took money to buy things at the store. If they could just get a garden started, they could raise potatoes and squash and pumpkins, but they had arrived too late in the year to plant a garden. They would have to spend wisely what money was left, and living frugally would help. The unnecessary items, no matter how much they were wanted, would have to stay at the store.

"And will he bring me a dolly, Mama?" Betsy asked in her direct, little-girl way. "I do so wish he would!"

Although Betsy had a china doll when they came over to America, it was a very small one. Their trunk and boxes filled so fast as they made their choices and packed necessities that there was no room for her larger doll, and so she left it with Bestemor Oleson, her grandmother on her father's side. Bestemor had promised to take good care of her. Since the tiny doll was the only plaything Betsy was allowed to bring from Norway, she had treasured it dearly. But then one of its legs broke. Tears still came to Betsy's eyes whenever she remembered the day it fell out of her apron pocket when she was helping pick up rocks. And more tears stung her eyes whenever she remem-

bered how George teased her about crying over such a small thing. He had said, "Why, the whole doll was only four inches long!"

Barbara understood fully how much Betsy wanted a new doll. She herself felt deprived of many of the familiar objects and scenes in their surroundings in the land they had left. She wondered sometimes whether she could endure the sadness and loneliness she felt when she thought of friends and relatives, and their home and the furnishings they had left behind in Norway.

Barbara looked steadily into Betsy's blue eyes as she spoke seriously, but kindly. "First, Papa must buy the things we need most. Maybe some day you will have a nice, new dokke...a new dolly...to play with. Maybe a bigger one that will not fit in your pocket, and so it will not fall out and break."

"Oh, Mama, I know one leg is broken off, and now I can't even find her. But I was so glad I could bring her with me, and now I miss her so much."

Maria sympathized with Betsy. "I know, Betsy. I remember how you cried and cried when she broke."

George joined the conversation again. "And when she got lost, you cried some more!" George made a long, sad face momentarily before he led the conversation away from Betsy's wish for a doll. Turning toward both his sisters, he spoke in his occasional "I know all about it" tone that Maria quickly recognized. "When I helped Papa hitch his oxen to the wagon, I asked him if I could go along. He said, 'No, George. When I am gone, you are the man of the family. Mama and the girls need you here.'"

George took a deep breath. Maria knew better than to interrupt her brother. He had a good memory when it came to a story. He would put in every detail that seemed important to him.

"Then I asked him, 'But why are you going, Papa? It is such a long way.'

"He said, 'Yes, and the okser, the oxen, are slow. But is that not better than if I walk all the way there and back? And if I did that, I would have to carry all the supplies on my back on the way home.'

"I asked him, 'What supplies, Papa? What do you need?'

"He said, 'Mama needs...' and he said all those things we just now said, that are all used up."

With a hint of impatience in her voice, Maria asked, "Well, what else did he say?"

"I asked him, 'How long will you be gone, Papa?'

"He said, 'With good traveling weather, it will take about three days. One to get there, one to come back, and a day between to buy the supplies and catch up on the news.' And then he said, 'It is good to know who is here. Maybe soon there will be enough children to start a school.' Then he said, 'Now I must be...' "

Mama brought George's story to a sudden end when she said, "If there is no trouble, Papa may be home before night."

"Trouble, Mama? What kind of trouble?" asked Maria, thinking that George surely liked to tell long stories.

Mama explained, "Papa never knows how long the old wagon wheels will hold together. Sometimes he has to repair them on the way. Sometimes he has to cut a piece of a stout tree branch to shape into a spoke to replace one on a wheel. And the trails are rough and devious as they lead around sloughs and ponds and along winding creeks to shallow places where they can be forded. Papa has to stop often to check the load, to make sure it is still there."

Maria added another reason. "And

the oxen need to rest and..."

Without waiting for Maria to finish, George suddenly asked, "Can we get some horses, Mama? It would be such fun to ride a horse...could Papa trade the oxen for horses?"

Barbara's face broke into one of her quick, seldom seen smiles as she asked, "George, do you see any horses grazing on this island, or across the wide prairie?"

"No, Mama. But I sure do wish I could ride one sometimes. Trader Wilkin has one, but he is gone so much. If we had some horses, I could ride bare-back like the Indians do. And I could give little Betsy rides..."

"I'm not little!" Betsy exploded as she frowned fiercely, annoyed with her brother.

"You're littler than me and Maria, little Betsy!"

Barbara brought the teasing to an end. "Nok sagt! Enough now! George, help me with these pails. And then all of you must gather some sticks and branches for a fire. We need to warm some water, to wash our soiled clothing."

"But not for baths, Mama," George tried. "We can take our baths in the lake today, can't we? It is sunny, and the air will not be cold at noon."

As much as Barbara would have liked that, knowing how dirty their feet were from the dirt floor of the dugout and from their playing outside, she said, "George, the water in the lake may still be as cold at noon as this water in the pails is this morning. But we will see. Do not even go near the lakeshore if I am not there, or Papa, when he comes home!"

"I won't, Mama," George promised as he lifted one of the pails too quickly, splashing water over Betsy's feet as she tried to reach into the pail to see how cold the water really was.

"I won't, either, Mama," Maria and Betsy chimed. Then Betsy moved closer to Maria and took hold of her hand, to go and pick up sticks for Mama.

How Papa Came to Choose Graham Lakes Country

As John Oleson rode home behind the oxen on his third day away from his family, he thought about the events that had brought them to this place, their new home in a new land — new to them.

First, he had heard about the international exhibition in Hyde Park, in London. Some of the people from his part of Norway attended it and, when they returned home, they told him about the interesting displays.

At about the same time, some of his friends began receiving "America letters" and sharing them. As these letters were passed from household to household, they spread a glowing picture of ways life in America was already proving better than in Norway. Those who sent the letters from their new country spoke of vast expanses of fertile land in contrast to the small percentage that could be cultivated in Norway. And John learned that in America, there were no heavy taxes to be paid to the state.

Not long after he heard about the international exhibition in London, John learned about another fair. Some New York businessmen had planned to hold a world's fair something like the London exhibition. It was held at the Crystal Palace in New York in 1853.

Because of one particular display at that world's fair, some of the farmers in Norway learned about the superior grains that could be grown in the fertile soil of Minnesota. A man named William LeDuc had gathered small grains: wheat, rye, oats, barley and corn. He said all of these could be grown there.

When John heard about the successful growth of grains in Minnesota soil, he decided that was what he wanted to do — go to America and try for a better life as a farmer. He and Barbara talked it over, and John eagerly began to construct a sturdy trunk that would withstand the trip by cart across part of Norway, by ship the rest of the way to America, and finally to this part of Minnesota.

John was just one of the many farmers who left their homelands in Europe to look for land in southern Minnesota. Many others from the eastern and northern United States also moved on west by the time the territory had been made a state in May of this very year.

To anyone who might have seen or talked with John Oleson as he rode home from Jackson, he would have seemed totally contented with his lot. He had heard that the jernbane, the railroad, would soon come across the southern part of the state. He hoped that when it came, it would be near enough to be of help to their settlement. And so, as he sat at the front of the wagon, his broad shoulders relaxed, he talked gently to the oxen as he gazed toward the trees that marked his land and his home — his hope and his dream.

Underneath all his seeming composure, there was another element — a purpose, a driving force — strong as could be. It was what kept him calm. It guided his every thought. It influenced his every decision. It had brought him this far, and he was determined to accomplish what he had set out to do here. No matter what difficulties came in the way, if it was at all within his power to do so, he would fulfill his dream to develop his own place in the new land he had chosen. He would make for himself and his family a mye bedre, a mye mer fruktbar gard — a much better, a much more productive farm than they had left in the homeland, no matter how hard it was to achieve.

For farming was the only way of life John knew. He realized that it would not be easy to make a productive farm here, starting with the hard work of converting the prairie to farmland that would produce the superior grains. He also knew that some of his near neighbors at Graham Lakes were planning to trap the abundant fur-bearing animals, and then trade the valuable furs for food and other necessary items. But John knew that he was basically a farmer, and he was healthy and strong and determined to make farming work here in Minnesota, where the wide expanses of land held rich, fertile soil beneath their tough prairie surface.

Maria Listens to the Prairie

Papa came home late that afternoon, all safe and sound. In the evening, after he put down the old newspaper he had been reading by candlelight, Mama moved the candle closer to her chair and read from the Bible. It wasn't long before the children were sound asleep.

The next morning, George and Maria gathered rocks along the sloping lakeshore and carried them up to the double tree. They knew the rocks would stay piled there better than on the shore where the waves moved them back and forth and sometimes, on very windy days, back into the lake. Maria had to ask George to help her roll and push some of the larger rocks to get them up to their pile.

Betsy helped, too. She picked up smaller ones, smooth-washed pebbles she gathered up into the skirt of her calico dress until she dumped them next to the other pile. They would fill in the spaces between the larger rocks in the foundation for the cabin that Papa planned to build. "But that will be a long time from now," he often said. "First we must break the prairie and plant some wheat."

Now, John paused to watch the children a little while. Then, when he said he was going to go over and break more prairie, Maria began a question, "But, Papa —" but George interrupted as he so often did, "But our island is not as big as a field. It is big enough to play on and to build a cabin on, but it would only make a very small field. Will you plant it all in wheat?"

"No, son. Here on the island there are too many trees. We can use them for shade in summer and for their wood, but we will make our field over there near the edge of the slough."

John Oleson reached out with one arm and pointed toward the mainland, as they all called it, saying, "George, do you see the place over there where the ground slopes up higher? There, it is farther from the slough and the lakes, and so it is also drier than much of the land here. And there are no trees — only prairie."

"Papa," Maria tried again, "does it hurt the prairie when you break it?"

"No, Maria. Not really," and he knit his heavy, dark brows together more closely as he thought how to explain so that Maria would understand. "The prairie cannot feel as we can. It has no mind, no heart."

"But, Papa, it must have. Otherwise, how can it sigh and cry one day and smile on us another day?"

John Oleson looked directly into Maria's eyes for a moment before he answered. Her words had made him think of Barbara, and he saw the image of Barbara in Maria's tall, thin figure. He saw the same bright blue eyes. But Maria had his own dark hair, though hers was longer. He said, "Maria, your thoughts are too old for your body. The prairie smiles when the sun shines on it, and it cries when the wind blows through it."

"Yes, Papa, and it is beautiful to watch. It keeps me company when I have nothing to do."

"It does? And how does it keep you company?"

"Sometimes I sit on the high ground behind the dugout and watch it."

"Hva ser du der min datter? What do you see there, my daughter?" Papa asked as his warm, brown eyes searched Maria's.

"I see the tall grass wave and bend in the wind, as the ocean waves did, back and forth, back and forth."

"You will remember that for a long time, Maria. When we left Norway, you were old enough to remember. Then it was the ocean. Now it is the prairie. What does it say to you?"

"Papa, it says wonderful things. It says, 'You are in a good land. Here there is water and wood, and there are fish and prairie chickens for food.'"

"Yes, Maria. And ducks and geese. We see them swim on the lakes. Does the prairie tell you more?"

"It says, 'When the summer is over and many pelicans land on the lakes to rest and to find food, the cold weather will soon come.'"

George felt a little too left out of the conversation, so he broke in with, "And that will happen soon! Does it tell you anything else?"

"It says, 'Here you can make a small farm like the one you had in Norway. But it will be easier to work.'"

John agreed. "Yes, that is true. The land is more flat and open. And what else does it say to you?"

"It says, 'When the storms come, you must hurry into the dugout. Or if your Papa is home and so the wagon is here, you can crawl under it to get out of the rain. And if the wind is very, very strong, you must help Mama hold down the rocks and branches on the wagon cover so it can not blow away.'"

"Vel, ja, det er alt sant. (Well, yes, that is also true.) The wagon cover keeps our trunk and my tools dry. There is not enough room for all those things in the dugout."

Betsy looked up at her father, her face showing surprise and a little fright. "Papa, do you think that will happen today? Will the wagon cover blow away?"

"No, Betsy. Today it is not windy. And now you'd best all be about gathering more sticks for Mama's cooking fire and more rocks for the foundation for our cabin."

As he watched his children move toward the trees where they would find the most sticks for kindling, John Oleson stood tall. He was proud of his children, in whom he saw hope — and especially now in Maria, their first-born. She was already beginning to show signs of maturing, not only in her body, but also in her mind. He saw hope in his children. He wished for each of them a peaceful future, free from the anxieties he knew their mother felt at times. He wished it were in his power to keep all his family, as well as their nearby relatives and friends, free from the troubles that might come if the Indians in the area became restless and belligerent. He knew that Barbara sometimes felt apprehensive, especially when he was not at home. He knew that the same concerns she felt were present for him, too, lurking beneath the surface calm like a spokelse, a presence, trying hard to disturb the purpose that drove him on from day to day. But he was determined not to let it prevent him from achieving his goal.

Getting the Plowshare Ready

George asked, "Will we make a foundation for the cabin today, Papa?"

"Not today, son. First I must break some more prairie. George, where is my special hammer and the piece of rail I brought along?"

"Here they are, Papa, next to this stump. I tried to break open a pebble, but it was too hard."

"Do not lose those tools, son. I need them to pound the worn edges of the plowshare flat. The iron lay is not very sharp when its edges are bent over."

"Papa," Maria asked, "what is the plowshare? What does that mean?"

"The plowshare is the part of the plow that cuts the furrow."

"But Papa, if you make it so sharp, it must hurt the prairie when the plow cuts it."

Sometimes when one of the children asked a question, their father's answer was like a lesson for all of them to hear and, that way, learn about this new land and the work that must be done on it. Now, his voice full of patience, Papa said, "Maria, the prairie sod is tough. The roots of the grasses and wildflowers and other plants grow into a tangle and make a thick mat that is almost solid. That is why I must break it with the plow, to cut it through and turn it over. Then, after the snow this winter and the rain next spring moisten and mellow it, the rich, dark loam will work up better."

George was looking forward to spring already. He said eagerly, "And then we can plant the wheat seed — and when you go to Jackson next fall, you can take our very own wheat to the mill to have it ground into flour."

Papa reminded George that there was no mill yet at Jackson. "The flour is brought there from Mankato, where there is a mill at the bend of the Minnesota River. Perhaps by the time we raise enough wheat, there will also be a mill at Jackson, on the Des Moines River. We will have to wait and see. There is not even a saw mill there yet. But remember that it takes a long time to make a farm here on the prairie."

George broke in with, "But, Papa, you said — when Maria said the land would be easier to work here, you said, 'Yes, that is true.'"

"Yes. Except for the stones in the lakes, there is not as much rocky land right here as there is in Norway. And more of the land is flat and can be used for fields. But the prairie has been here for years and years. I have been told that it takes about two years to get a piece of prairie ready to use as a field so that we can expect to raise a crop. And I can believe that."

"But the oxen are so slow, Papa. Couldn't we break more prairie each day if we had horses?"

"Son, the okser, the oxen, are slow but they are strong. Strong enough to pull the plow through even the tangled 'shoe-string' weed."

"But horses are faster. Cousin Howie said so. His father borrows trader Wilkin's horses sometimes, when Wilkin is not away trading with the Indians."

"Yes. He does." Papa continued pounding the edges of the lay flat as he said, "And hester, horses, would be faster. And more fun for you when you are tall enough to jump on one and ride it. And with two horses, our one-lay plow would turn about an acre a day, or maybe two if the horses were very strong."

Betsy tried to follow the talk about horses and plowing. Maria thought that so far, having horses made sense, until her father continued, "But if we didn't get rain the sod would be very dry and tough. Then we would need four horses to pull the plow. Four horses, one man walking the furrow between the handles to keep the lay in the ground and keep it going straight, and feed for four horses. Our oxen will do our work just fine, if not as fast. And since I bought them at the end of our journeys by rail and then by boat, they have served us well to bring us to our new home — and now, to turn the soil."

Papa laid the piece of rail and the special hammer down on a stump near the dugout. Then he stretched his back and arms as he stood up tall and straight and said, "Now I believe the plow is ready. I must get the oxen and get on with my work."

As John walked behind the oxen and the plow toward the prairie that would become a field, he reflected that all the land would soon look very different. It was changing even now. He knew that surveyors had worked in Nobles County for a few days in 1852, and again later that same year after the line between Iowa and Minnesota was established.

Once he set the lay into the sod his efforts were directed toward keeping it at an even depth and plowing the furrows straight. Thinking about straight lines reminded him that a surveying party had visited Nobles County again just recently.

When the Olesons and their neighbors came to Graham Lakes, they chose their sites and stayed on them to establish their farms and homes. It was not yet possible to file claims at a land office. Now that surveyors were working in the county, John hoped he and his neighbors would have no trouble holding onto their property later on, when the township and section lines were run and more settlers came.

He knew that even now others were drifting into southwestern Minnesota. He knew that, though he and his neighbors had chosen land near these two beautiful lakes, others had settled along the Des Moines River where both vatn and ved, water and wood, were also available. And he knew that there were small settlements in Jackson, Cottonwood and Martin counties to the east of Nobles County, and some up in Murray County to the north where there were also lakes.

He thought, Perhaps it is good that we came ahead of many who will no doubt follow. Once the jernbane comes, many towns will be started in Nobles County and the others around it.

Taming the Prairie

That afternoon while John worked in the field, Barbara kept the children at home. They sat in the shade of an oak tree while she taught them their lessons. Even Betsy at the age of four wanted to learn to read, and George liked to do his "figures and numbers" as he called them. But his mind was not on his lessons.

George welcomed the shout from the mainland. The children knew that Papa was cupping his hands in front of his mouth and calling, "Hallo! George! Kom hit og hjelper meg naa. Come over here and help me now!"

Barbara wondered if her husband realized how gladly George abandoned his books. She watched him as he crossed the narrow neck of land by which they left the island. He was thin and growing taller, going through one of those growth spurts, but he had lots of energy, especially for playing and exploring. But he even preferred helping his father to doing the lessons on a good day.

As she watched George run on toward the field, Barbara thought, Today is a good day. The water does not cover the low strip of land. When the heavy rains come, it will be under water and we here on our island will be cut off from the others. Sometimes she felt at a disadvantage not to live nearer to other families, especially here where she didn't know the Indians well enough to trust them as neighbors. She didn't know what to expect from them.

When he saw George coming, John Oleson waited in the near corner of the field he was shaping. George ran faster and stopped there in grass trampled flat by the oxen.

John said, "Son, you can help me now. Sometimes the plow lifts the chunks of sod so that they don't turn over all the way. Instead, they stand on edge. If we don't lay them down, with the dirt side up, the field will be harder to work up in the spring."

"What should I turn them over with, Papa? Did you bring along a tool to use? Or should I run back to the island and find a forked stick?"

"Your hands will do very well, George. Walk in the furrows, and put your mind on what you are doing."

A twinkle in Papa's eyes brought an inquisitive look on George's face, but John turned around and set the oxen in motion before another question surfaced. George started to follow a yard or two behind his father. He tried to keep up, but when many chunks stood on end in one row, he fell behind. Sometimes the roots and stems tore at his hands, and he soon felt his arms and back aching from lifting the heavy blocks of sod.

George was just beginning to wonder if horses wouldn't somehow do a better job of this work, when John came back up the next row. George looked down the row. The furrow was straight and black but there were more of those heavy, solid chunks of sod stubbornly standing on edge. He wished he could lay them flat as easily as he could a row of dominoes. If only they were closer together and evenly spaced, and not so heavy...

Just then Barbara and Maria came to his rescue. Leaving Betsy at the edge of the field, Barbara told George he could sit by her and have some cold venison and a biscuit while he watched her. "But be sure to stay right by her. Don't wander off to explore in the tall grass, this time. Stay right there by Betsy, where we can see you both!"

Barbara and Maria stepped into John's last two furrows and tackled the stubborn chunks of sod. Maria tried to set a rhythm as though she were jumping rope or doing something else less demanding. She made up a rhyme: Grass side down, dirt side up/down one row, then back up. But it wasn't that easy and it wasn't that fast. She soon lost all thought of pleasant rhymes and rhythms as she leaned over and struggled to turn the heavy, clumsy lumps. She tried to keep up with her mother in the other furrow.

Mama Joins the Children in Their Songs

When the sun started to slide toward the horizon, the tired children and their mother walked quickly back to their island. Barbara, getting ready to make supper, wondered where the rest of that smoked venison went. She knew she had left it on the broad tree stump that served as a table in the dugout. Not wanting to frighten the children, and knowing that John would not want her to worry, she tucked the question into the back of her mind as she listened to their songs.

First they sang in English. Already in Norway the school Maria and George attended had taught the main language of the new world to which so many Norwegians were going, and Betsy had picked up the words from them.

Barbara listened.

> "Baa, baa, little lamb, have you any wool?
> Yes, yes, dear child, I have a body full!
> Sunday clothes for father and Sunday clothes for mother,
> and two pair of socks for my tiny little brother."

When Barbara started the song again, but in their native tongue, the children joined her.

> "Bae, bae, lille lam, har du noe ull?
> Ja, ja, Kjaere barn, jeg har Kroppen full!
> Sondags-klaer til far og sondags-klaer til mor,
> og to par stromper til bitte lille bror."

Hearing the children singing the Norwegian words immediately gave Barbara a twinge of what she called ensomhet, loneliness for the old home and family and friends left behind. She thought perhaps it was the old, familiar language that had been their native tongue that brought on the loneliness now, just as naturally as the old words still came to mind for her and John before the English words did.

Barbara thought then of the song the Hauglands from Spring Grove sang when a group of immigrants gathered to visit at Rochester. The Olesons were pausing there a few hours to rest and to ask about the land ahead, and what to expect in the next lap of their journey.

The Hauglands said that the song was composed by other immigrants from Norway out of loneliness for the old country. Now Barbara surprised herself by remembering the original words and melody as she sang a few verses for the children:

> "Kan du glemme gamle Norge?
> Aldri jeg det glemme kan,
> som med stolte klippeborge
> er og blir mitt fodeland.

> "La da kun tanke sveve;
> det kan aldri falle tungt.
> Ma for nordmenn lenge leve
> gamle Norge, evig ungt!"

When the children begged her to teach them the song, too, she sang it in English:

> "How can you forget old Norway,
> Land of rock and narrow fjord,
> Where the mountains are like castles,
> Stand like sentinels on guard?

> "How can you forget old Norway
> And its narrow fjords so grand,
> In and out between the mountains?
> 'Tis my own, my native land!"

With those last lines, tears filled her eyes. She paused just long enough for Maria to notice her mother's sadness and wonder about it. But Barbara had sung only those two stanzas before Papa came home from the field, tired but ready for supper.

John also noticed the tears and wondered what had brought on the sad mood this time. It pleased him to see that Maria seemed to understand and sympathize with Barbara. At least, she had quietly set about helping get the supper on.

Pangs of Loneliness on the Prairie

Early the next day, Papa went alone to the mainland to continue the hard work of taming the prairie. Barbara, up before the children, busied her hands with the mending, but her mind was active with other thoughts. One was that the children's songs were a good thing for them and for her, too. Songs went a long way toward easing the loneliness, here on the prairie. Not that there weren't enough people nearby. Her own family kept her busy enough. But there were times when she looked out over the prairie and wondered what the other women were doing and whether they were experiencing the same feelings as she was. Sometimes she felt joy, sometimes contentment, now and then surprise. But also, now and then, she felt a great deal of uncertainty and, even more often, a deep ensomhet, a deep loneliness.

Barbara felt that some of the loneliness was for the homeland, the old country. They had had a modest farm, but its location made hard work necessary. There were so many rocks and there was no flat, open expanse of land to make farming easier. Here there was flat, open land with rich soil waiting beneath the sod if the farmers were persistent in preparing it for raising crops. Yet Barbara missed the feelings of solidity and character the fjords and the rocky outcroppings gave the old farm.

And there were times when she missed her slekter, her relatives who had not left the homeland. She missed her aged father who did not care to make the voyage. He was content where he was. And sometimes, especially in the evenings when the family sat together in the dugout while one or the other read from the old newspapers or the Bible or the storybooks the children preferred, a vision would break into Barbara's thoughts, a vision so familiar, yet distant. She saw her own far, her father, standing by the hearth in his home in the fishing village, playing his violin. Standing straight, head tilted toward the chin rest of the instrument, his graying hair and beard adding dignity to his posture as he closed his eyes and drew the bow across the strings. Like the lark that soars higher and higher and sings its heart out before it gives up its life, her father poured his whole heart, his whole being, into the music so full of warmth and feeling and all emotions familiar to the heart.

When she saw that Maria was awake, Barbara wondered if Maria would some day learn to play the old songs, maybe even on the same violin the children's bestefar, their grandfather, played so tenderly. But the loneliness was still there, and even deeper for having thought about it.

Barbara Thinks About Their Trip Across Minnesota

Late one day, as she went about her work, Barbara thought about her sister-in-law Betsey Kushman, John's sister.

The Kushmans had also made the voyage from Norge (Norway) in the early spring of 1858 and on the same ship with the Olesons. Early spring with its fair weather held more promise of a smooth voyage than summer or fall did.

Soon after arriving in New York Harbor, the two families traveled by train across the eastern states. They were able to go all the way to Chicago and beyond, to where the railroads ended at Galena, very near the big river. There, both families joined others who traveled up the Mississippi from Galena on a stern-wheel paddle boat. They could have traveled by water all the way up to St. Paul, as there was a daily line of steam packets operating. But the boats made many stops along the way and, by the time they reached a landing across from Winona, Minnesota, Betsey felt that she couldn't travel on the water another day. She had whispered to Barbara, "My time is very near. We must find a place to stay for a while." They found a small settlement on the east bank of the river.

After saying their goodbyes to the Kushmans, including many wishes for the best of health and a safe birth, the Olesons and their belongings were ferried across the water. First, though, Papa told Uriah, "We will see you again after your baby is born and you can travel on. Look for us in southwestern Minnesota. Inquire along the way at Owatonna and again at Mankato."

Uriah asked, "How much farther do you plan to go after you reach Mankato?"

"Keep in mind that we will be looking for two lakes. When you reach Jackson you will not have much farther to go; ask directions again when you are there. There are several lakes west of Jackson. The two I have in mind are called Graham Lakes — East Graham and West Graham. We will go that way. Perhaps we can find those lakes. We hope to see you there. Gaa med Gud; go with God."

After more fond embraces and gentle words and abundant tears, especially between Barbara and Betsey, the Kushmans walked slowly away from the landing.

Once the ferry reached the west bank of the Mississippi River, the Olesons' belongings were unloaded. Then Papa bought the covered wagon and the yoke of oxen, near the town called Winona. They loaded their heavy trunk and numerous boxes and bags into the wagon. Not caring to go upstate to St. Paul, John started out west toward Rochester. Although Betsy slept much of the way, making the trip seem shorter for her as she cuddled next to either her mother or her sister, it seemed to Maria that they had ridden in that wagon forever when they paused at Rochester to rest and to visit with other folks gathered there.

Some of them had settled already; others were moving on. From a Mr. Haugland, John learned of a Norwegian settlement at Spring Grove. When he asked about it, he was told that it had been established in 1856, or perhaps earlier. Haugland said there was already a church at Spring Grove. It was known as the Norwegian Ridge Lutheran Church, and services were held there regularly. He said that a pastor who had also come from Norway had been conducting the services.

"That is tempting," Papa told Haugland. "We could end our long journey and settle here. But it is my feeling that in a short time we would only move on again."

Haugland asked, "Then where do you plan to stop, John?"

"I have a strong desire to choose land in an entirely new country where we would be starting a new life. We have

27

come far, but this part of the state is no longer the frontier. Now that we have our ox team and wagon, we may as well push on."

Barbara asked, "Where is Spring Grove, John?"

"We are well past Spring Grove. We would be backtracking toward the Mississippi River again. Spring Grove is almost at the Minnesota-Iowa border, in southeast Minnesota. The Graham Lakes are nearer the southwest corner."

And so, after their visit at Rochester, the Oleson family went on west. At each place that seemed to be the nucleus of a settlement, they stopped to rest and inquire the way across the state to where John knew Nobles County had been designated by the legislature and included on maps only the previous year.

They finally arrived in the Graham Lakes country by the middle of July in 1858. Papa's first task was to build a jordhytte, a dugout, on the site he chose, the island in one of the lakes. He knew there was not enough time to begin working up the land to make a field and also to cut down trees and trim them for logs for a cabin, but a dugout could be built quickly and it would provide shelter then and warmth when winter came on.

When the Kushmans joined their relatives at the Graham Lakes, they brought a gift of smoked dyrekjott, venison, from friends they had made in Wisconsin. They were happy to share the gift. Each family put the venison away in their salt barrels in a corner of their dugouts. But an even greater gift they shared was the presence of the newest settler and relative, tiny Ann Kushman. She had been born in Wisconsin just two days after they said farewell to the Olesons and the Olesons moved on west. Barbara realized that Ann was almost three months old now.

Pioneer log home of Elling Enger near Spring Grove, Minnesota.

Barbara Thinks About Her Neighbors

Barbara's thoughts moved on to others in their settlement, those who were not related to them but were becoming good venner, good friends and good neighbors. There was Ann Bumgardner, the wife of George, a farmer. They were of the same ages as John and Barbara, but they had come from Bavaria. They had crossed the Atlantic on the same ship, in the spring of 1858, but the Bumgardners and the Hertwinkles, also from Bavaria, stayed close together and didn't mingle much with others on the voyage. Some passengers said it was because those two families all spoke the same language, but it was not Norwegian. But now, here by the lakes, Ann Bumgardner's oldest, Henrietta or "Etta" as everyone there called her, and Maria, the same age, liked to play and read together whenever they could. They were becoming good friends. The language difference was no barrier for them. Each had learned a little English in school before leaving Europe, and both had learned more as they crossed the eastern states in English-speaking country. The words from their native tongue still came easily now and then, but the girls did not use them as often as their parents did.

Thomas and William Hertwinkle and Marie, their sister, were older than the other children by several years. The only boys close to George's age were his cousins Howie and William Kushman, who were both closer to little Betsy's age. Ann Bumgardner's youngest, "Maria B." as she was called to distinguish her from Maria Oleson, was only a year old, and her Wilmetto or "Wilmy" was six.

The older Hertwinkle young folks had a young cousin Monica, daughter of John and Joanna Hertwinkle, also from a farm in Bavaria. Monica was their first child. She, like Ann Kushman, was born in Wisconsin. Monnie was an infant when her family arrived at the lakes.

"Uncle Thomas" Hertwinkle, Joanna said, was from Bavaria, too. He was William and John Hertwinkle's younger brother and he was twenty-four. In Bavaria he had worked for others as a farm laborer, since he had no family of his own.

Then there were the single men: John Bell, Thomas Marks, and Henry Jordan, the three trappers from the East. Barbara knew that trapping was very necessary for some to live because farming here was so slow. Some trapped to sell or trade furs in order to have food. Barbara thought perhaps it was that way for those three. She hoped the small amount of money she and John had been able to keep in reserve since they left Norway would last until their first crop of grain could be harvested. Otherwise, it might come to that for John, too. He might have to give up farming and take up trapping to have something to trade for food, to keep them all from starving.

Another member of the new community was George Wilkin, born in Wisconsin long before any of this group of settlers pioneered through that state. He was an Indian trader. He had no family, at least not with him. He spent most of his time trading with the Indians, and he felt that by now he knew them quite well.

There were also the three Eavens folks — William and Maria, and Thomas. Barbara thought that Thomas must be their grown son. She recalled that they also came from her homeland, but not from her part of the country.

The Irish McFarlane brothers, George and Henry, were both around thirty. They were good neighbors on the mainland ever since they had joined the group. They didn't have any womenfolk with them yet, though George said he had sent for his wife.

And then there was George Evert, born in Maine, and Henry Hanson, born in Tennessee, both grown men older than her John, Barbara thought. But they were traders and they were away much of the time. She knew that the trappers and traders had been in the territory the longest except for the Indians, of course. It seemed that they had been here from the beginning. And somehow, thinking about that brought a tremor of fear. Barbara did not yet feel entirely at ease, knowing the Indians were so near.

Barbara's reverie was broken by the children's shouts as Papa came back to the island following the oxen and the plow, but no longer setting the lay into the ground.

After supper, Betsy climbed up onto her father's lap. Her unruly blonde curls made a striking contrast against his dark skin and beard as she rested her head on his chest. She could hardly stay awake long enough to hear the first verses of the seventh chapter of Matthew, the ones about the mote.* George wondered what a mote was. Maria thought of the moat around a castle. She remembered her grandpa telling her about moats around castles, when they were still living in Norway.

John read more of Matthew 7. Barbara listened intently as he read from verse 9: "...or what man is there of you, whom if his son ask bread, will he give him a stone?" and the verses that followed — a "golden rule," so to speak. Then still thinking about motes, the children went to bed.

A little later, settled in their narrow bed against one wall of the dugout, John and Barbara talked of the day's events, their work, their children, and their neighbors. Barbara told her husband about the missing venison.

Maria, not yet asleep, heard her father say reassuringly, "You know there are Indians all around us. They have been good neighbors and helpers. If you were not at home when

*The Holy Bible, King James Version, Matthew 7: 3-5 and verse 9 ff.

they came to ask for food, they had a right to help themselves."

Barbara was not easily reassured. She said, "But it frightens me. When were they here, even in the dugout where they found the venison I left out? And will they come again, for more food?"

In the silence of the night, Maria wondered if Papa forgot that the venison was a gift their relatives had brought from Wisconsin. She fell asleep thinking how good a big pot of venison stew would taste.

Loneliness Brings a Visitor

The next morning George went along with Papa to the
field. Maria watched Betsy, and Mama washed clothes again.
Mama liked to have things neat, including her children.
Since there was not much of a house to keep tidy, and even
then it didn't stay tidy for very long with the dirt floors and
the dirt and strands of grass the wind sometimes blew in,
she spent her abundant energy on the washings. And Maria
knew that she and Betsy would be next. Mama said she
would wash their hair when they bathed in the lake, when
the air was warmed a little more in the middle of the day.
"Soon," Mama had said, "the lake will be much too cold."

Maria jumped a little when she saw movement down at
the narrow neck of land. Before she fell asleep the night
before, she had heard her parents speaking of the Indians.
Now she strained to see who was coming.

But Barbara quickly recognized her sister-in-law. Though
they did not come to the island often, Betsey and Uriah
were their nearest neighbors. The piece of prairie Uriah was
breaking was adjacent to John's. No doubt the men were
visiting right now, there where their "squatter's rights"
brought them together as they worked.

Aunt Betsey carried Ann in her arms as she trudged
through the fallen leaves to meet Barbara halfway.

"Howie and William are helping their father, just as
George is helping John," she said to Barbara as she chose a
stump to sit on near the dugout. "William is small, but he
wants to help, too."

"I'm glad you could come," Barbara greeted her sister-in-
law as she seated herself on another stump. "But what
brings you today? It isn't often you can come all the way
over here just to visit."

"Oh, I just felt a little lonesome for you, and I had a little
dream last night. It made me wonder if you were all right

over here."

"Oh, Betsey, I was feeling a little ensomhet yesterday, too. When I look out across the prairie and see nothing but wide expanses of grass one way and our clumps of trees almost shutting out the view the other way, I think about all the others in our little settlement. And I wonder how they are, and if life will ever be easier for us here."

"When I think like that, Uriah scolds me. He says not to give up haap, hope. Hope will pull us through, he keeps telling me."

"Hope and hard work, and faith that it will all work out," Barbara said. Then she remembered what else her sister-in-law had said. She asked, "Betsey, why did you wonder if we were all right? What did you dream about?"

"It wasn't so much the dream." Aunt Betsey lowered her voice as she went on. "Something else happened. The prairie hen Uriah had dressed out for me before he went to the field was hanging there, ready for me to cook it, when he left. After I got Ann up and fed, I went to get the hen. But it was gone. And it couldn't have been taken by anything but a two-legged creature about five feet tall."

"I know what you mean. I left some smoked dyrekjott out when I took a lunch to the field yesterday. When I got home it was gone, too — right off the slab table in the dugout!"

"That gives me a strange feeling. If the Indians come around and help themselves when we are not at home, what else will they do?"

"John put me at ease about that. He said it could as well have been the other way around. They were here first. They showed us how to find meat and how to live in this country. They helped us all they could, even though we invaded their land. He said, 'If you had been home, they would have asked first, in their own way.'"

Aunt Betsey told Barbara that during their stay in

Wisconsin, they had heard of some
restlessness among the Sioux. "The
pakkhusforvalter, the storekeeper,
said he feared that the Indians
want to keep us out of their land."
   "Yes, Betsey, we've heard that,
too. The Indians are already displeased because so many whites
are coming in, ever since the treaty
of 1851."

Betsey seemed to have a hard
time believing that. She burst out, "But it is no longer their
land!"
   Barbara tried to calm her. "John said they are like the
deer that come cautiously to the edge of the woods, but are
easily frightened away. He says we should want them to
trust us." But then she asked, "But do they think they can
keep the West from developing?"
   "I don't know about that, but others told us that the
Indians want to clear the country of us. They want to send
us all back to the east side of the big river or drepe us, kill
us, if necessary. They believe it is fair to remove us from the
land we took from them."
   Aunt Betsey's remarks were the last thing Barbara needed
to hear, but now she realized that her own fears were
understandable, and that her sister-in-law must feel much
the same as she did about the Indians. She asked, "But you
heard of no specific attacks before you came to join us
here?"
   "If there were any, the news had not yet reached us. Or
perhaps we missed it. We were busy with the baby and,
soon after, our departure."
   As the women talked, Maria and Betsy tired of picking up
rocks for the foundation they couldn't visualize. They came

closer to where their mother and aunt sat talking. Maria
took Ann from Aunt Betsey and started to walk away toward
the shade of the trees.

"Stay close by, Maria," Aunt Betsey called. "Do not wander off. I do not want to let little Ann out of my sight."

Maria thought there was a bit of a sharp edge in Aunt
Betsey's voice, but she hadn't heard enough of the women's
conversation to be frightened. She did as she was told and
sat on the leaf-strewn grass near them. Her sister sat down
next to her. The three girls played, "Here's the church,
here's the steeple, open the door and out come all the people." Holding four-month-old Ann in her lap, Maria helped
her shape her hands, but it was hard to do. Ann didn't
understand what she was supposed to do. Betsy was
pleased that she herself could make a very good church and
steeple.

Next they tried, "Simon says thumbs up," but that was
impossible for Ann. And Maria had to jump up and down as
she held her young cousin. Finally Barbara handed Maria a
white linen handkerchief from her apron pocket and Maria
started them playing, "Where is Ann? There she is!" and
"Where is Betsy? There she is!" The handkerchief felt good
as the smooth, cool square slid down over their faces, and
the game brought smiles and giggles from all three girls.

Later in the day Aunt Betsey picked Ann up and, hugging
her sister-in-law and nieces, said her goodbyes. Knowing it
could be spring before she would see the Olesons again,
she called out, "Take care!" as she started back toward the
neck of the island. She waited at the fields until her husband and sons were ready to go home. Then she told Uriah
that Howie and Willie could walk home with her while he
drove their oxen home.

Uriah watched until his wife and children were hidden
from his view by the wild bluestem that was as high as a

horse's back. Then he had to trust that they would be safe until he, too, would reach home.

When they had all gone, George guessed that Trader Wilkin must be using his horses himself, because Uncle Uriah was using the oxen that day. George was intrigued by the thought that Mr. Wilkin must have many interesting times in his life, dealing with the Indians. He almost wished he could ride along with Wilkin sometime instead of following his father in the field. But he didn't ask to.

Moses in the Bulrushes?

Before the coldest months, John took time to make a sturdy door for the dugout. He had known all along that the pieces of quilt would not keep out the cold wind and the snow.

First, he had George help him split a slender tree trunk into lengths to form a simple wood frame against the top and sides of the opening, where the sod blocks would give just enough to set the frame securely in place.

On another day, he cut slabs from some thicker logs and used them to make a door that would keep out the winter weather much better than the quilt could.

Soon after the door was hinged to the frame, winter came and the outside work stopped. The floor of the cabin was very cold then, and the Olesons stayed as close to the wood stove as they could.

On those winter evenings, as they sat together in the dugout while they talked or read or sang, it was not unusual for the candles to go out and leave them in darkness. Either the drafts were strong enough to put out a candle's flame, or a lamp would be extinguished by a large moth attracted by the light. When that happened, everyone seemed a little jumpy until the candle or the lamp was lit again.

The days were short and the nights seemed long, but, in time, spring followed and the field work resumed.

Suddenly it was June. One day that was like all others, George wondered when the field would be ready to plant. But then he remembered what Papa had said: "It takes about two years to make a field out of a piece of prairie, especially when it is not started until late in the season."

Mama insisted on bader, baths, toward the end of that day. The air was warm and the sun had not yet gone down. These days in June were long and mild, and usually very pleasant. Here in the sandy-bottomed pool between the point of land and the fallen tree trunk was a good place to bathe. And there was much more room than in the dugout.

First, Mama helped Maria wash her long, dark hair. Then she turned her attention to Betsy while Maria finished her own bath. Soon Maria, dressed now, dried Betsy and helped her dress while Mama washed her own long hair and then took her own bath.

Just as Maria reached out to hand the towel to Mama, a slight movement out on the lake caught her attention. Maria clutched Betsy's hand. Mama couldn't reach the towel. Seeing the look on Maria's face, she asked, "What is it, Maria? What did you see? Is someone else here?"

The girls took a few steps toward Mama with the towel. Maria whispered, "Mama, there is a canoe out there near the slough, and there is a dark-skinned person sitting in it. I think it is an Indian. I wonder — was he watching us?" She shivered.

Barbara turned to face the girls. Drying herself hurriedly and pulling her plain cotton dress down over her still-damp body, Barbara whispered back, "If it is an Indian, Maria, he will not harm us. Papa said not to be afraid. And do not frighten Betsy."

As they started up the worn path back to the dugout, they

met Papa and George coming to the warm, clear pool to wash the field dirt from their tired bodies. George could hardly bend over any more, but he knew the water would feel good on his aching legs and arms and back as he cupped his hands and dipped it over himself.

Barbara was still trying to draw her thin, light brown hair back and up from her face and neck. She caught most of it in the tortoise-shell comb that held most of it slightly puffed at the back while wisps of it fell softly around her neck. As she passed George she said, "Don't forget your neck and ears, son." As she passed John, she gave an emphatic nod toward the slough. Then the three women of the family made their way back to the dugout together, hand in hand.

That evening Maria was asked to read from the book with the blue cover, the old book called Bible Stories for Children. George wanted her to read about Samson. He thought it would be good to be so strong. But somehow, to Maria, the story of Moses in the basket in the water seemed more fitting to that day's events. Even Betsy seemed to sense feelings running high when she prayed, "Jesus bless us all...and keep us...safe...from the...," but she didn't finish it before she fell sound asleep in her father's broad, comfortable lap.

Maria didn't find it so easy to sleep. Her mind held the picture she saw that day on the lake, near the slough. It was the silhouette of a dark Indian, probably copper-colored like those few she had seen. He was sitting in a canoe, lifting the paddles gently, then quietly and smoothly pulling them through the water as the canoe slipped away over the lake. Maria thought that must have been the motion that caught her attention.

Maria was aware that her body was changing, filling out. She hoped he was far enough away not to notice, when she was drying herself and getting dressed. She was embarrassed enough when George was in the dugout while she dressed.

Not able to forget about the Indian, she asked, "Why are the lakes here called Graham Lakes? Did the Indians name them?"

Mama answered, "I only know they were called that by people we talked with as we came here."

Papa said, "In Jackson the clerk at the butikk, the store, asked where we were living. When I told him we were here in Graham Lakes country, he said he had heard of the lakes. Another man in the store said they were named Graham Lakes already in 1838 when Joseph Nicollet and John Fremont and others made an expedition through here. They mapped and named many features of the land."

Mama commented, "I wonder how the land was different then, when they came through."

Papa's answer was, "It all belonged to the Indians. They hunted and fished, but they did not change the land as much as the white people are changing it now."

Maria thought it would be wonderful to know as much as the men Papa talked to in the store...and the explorers, too. She hoped some day she would see a map that would show how the land looked then.

With her thoughts on maps and books, she fell asleep without thinking again about the Indian in the canoe.

Getting Two Jobs Done at Once

The rest of June went by. The days seemed to be alike. Papa and George worked in the field, still taming the prairie to get it ready for the wheat seed. Papa used a small wooden drag to work the soil up finer. Where larger chunks persisted, George broke them up with a  garden fork. The field was closer to being ready for the seed wheat, but it would be too late for a crop this year.

Sometimes Mama and Maria helped. Most days, though, they stayed close to the dugout, and Betsy was always by their side.

One day in early July, when John and George were working in the field, Barbara and her daughters walked all the way from the island and around the end of the slough to where the Bumgardners and the Hertwinkles were already building simple log cabins. Barbara wanted to see how the work was coming along.

When Maria and Etta found each other, they were given permission to go for a walk if they stayed close to where the men were working on the cabins. The two looked enough alike to be sisters. Etta also had long, dark hair falling over her shoulders and down her back. She was about the same height as Maria and the same build. They were the same age. But Etta did not have the deep dimple that appeared on Maria's right cheek when she smiled.

The girls munched on ripe black raspberries at the edge of the woods as they walked. Watching the men work, Maria began to see how the foundation of their own cabin would be set up. There would be four big, flat boulders for supporting the four corners. Then, between them, the large rocks would be piled on each other in rows as straight and even as was possible, while small rocks would fill in the gaps.

Maria said, "So that's how it is done! I can see we will need many more rocks before Papa can build our foundation!"

Etta said, "Maybe you could use some help from us, too. We can start our cabin now because our Papa and Mr. Hertwinkle have the help of the two older boys. Thomas is seventeen and William is thirteen. Their sister Marie helps, too. And their Uncle John Hertwinkle is young and strong. He is helping all of us. And when Monnie is a little older, their Uncle John and Uncle Thomas will start their own cabins and all our men will help them."

"It is good that you have their help now. Are your fields ready, too?" Maria asked.

"No, not yet," Etta answered. "But my sisters are still small and cannot help in the field. So Papa helps the neighbors a few days and then they help Papa a few days. And so it all gets done a little faster but a little later, too."

"But they are getting two jobs done at once — building their log cabins and breaking prairie. It seems like it is taking forever for Papa to get one small field ready. And there is never time for him to help Mama get a small garden patch ready near the dugout."

"But this is still our first whole summer here," Etta reminded Maria. "There should be time this fall to build your cabin. At least my Papa says so."

"And my Papa says, 'If we don't get a cabin built this summer, there are friendly Indians who hunt and fish near here. Maybe they will help us build one before the cold winds come.'"

"Doesn't that send shivers up your back, though?"

"What — talking about the cold winds?"

"No, Maria. Thinking about the Indians helping build your home."

"But Papa said they will help us if we help them. We are living on their land, he says, and it is harder every day for them to find food."

"I heard some of the men talking about the Indians one day. They called them 'the red men who steal.' They said, 'It is wrong of them to take the meat from our tables.'"

"After he read from the Bible last night, Papa said that when men talk that way about the Indians, they should take the beam out from their own eyes before they try to cast out the mote from the other men's eyes."

With a little giggle, Maria went on. "George thinks of a beam as a huge piece of wood like some he saw at the mills in the East. Like one that would hold up a whole roof of a cabin. It would be hard to have one in your eye!"

"I know, Maria. It is hard to understand. But I think your Papa means that we shouldn't blame the Indians or find fault with them when we have done all we have to make life hard for them."

"Yes. Like moving onto their land, killing the wild game they depend on for food, or driving it away because of all the activity with so many people moving in," Maria said.

"Well, if they do come to help your Papa build your cabin, that will give us something different to watch, all right!"

At that moment William Hertwinkle, Jr. called to them. "Etta," he shouted over the noise, "bring Maria with you and go back to your dugout now. Maria's mama says it is time to start back home."

"All right, Willie. We hear you," Etta called out. "We're going."

The Oleson Cabin Is Built

August came to an end. John had the field all ready so he could work it up quickly just once more in the Spring and then plant the wheat. He even found time to clear a small spot near the dugout for a garden for Barbara. But it was too late to plant and harvest now. It would have to wait, even if it meant they would have to use up much of what money was left to buy potatoes and other supplies for the winter once again.

"But it is not too late to start our cabin," John Oleson said.

And so the days of early fall were filled with activity. The children seemed to enter into all of it with more energy, more interest. The three young Olesons gathered more rocks, making a contest of who could carry the largest one, or at other times who could roll one the farthest.

Before the walls of the cabin were built, John saw to it that a space was dug out first, so that later, when the slab floor was put in, there would be a space below it, like a very shallow basement.

"Why do you want a hole beneath the cabin, John?" Uriah asked.

"I have heard," John answered, "that a crawl space makes a convenient place to store the potatoes and other foods that keep better in a cool place, and without freezing. It only needs to be about four feet deep. We can use some of the rocks the children have gathered to shore up the sides of the space before the large corner boulders are set in place for the cabin itself to rest on."

While Uriah and John dug the dirt away and out of the hole, John said, "Then, when we lay the floor, we will saw a part of it so that we can lift it and reach the potatoes, etc., down there, without going outside when it is very cold."

"You plan to make an outside entry to it, too?"

"I believe I will. Later on, if we get a few hens so we can have fresh eggs, they can get in and out from the outside and be warmer, and safer from the foxes and other predators that might go after them."

"That sounds like a good plan, John. I wish I had thought of it before we built our cabin."

The work of building the Oleson cabin soon progressed at a faster pace. The men cut down trees and trimmed the trunks and large branches for logs for the walls. The children dragged the branchy tops and ends to a separate pile. They could be used later for firewood, after the leaves dried and fell off. The men dragged the logs to the cabin site and notched them to set them securely at the corners where the cabin walls met. Papa used the oxen to pull the larger logs.

The conversation among those who spoke one another's language had much to do with the trees they were cutting down and trimming up.

Uriah guessed that there must be about 75 acres of timber nearby.

John said, "I think we have almost 10 acres of it right here on our island. The oak and ash and hackberry are easy to tell apart. The oaks branch out so strangely, almost as if bent and tangled by the winds."

The Foss log cabin was built in Ottertail County in the 1860s.

"And the hackberry trees have straight, sturdy trunks," Uriah said, "but the bark and leaves are different from the other trees."

"I have heard that some loggers favor the oak. When we passed by the Big Woods, that was the talk. Many of the trees there were oak."

"Perhaps it is the builders that favor the oak. But for furniture, as for a table top or a bedstead, there is much beauty in the hackberry. When a finish is applied to it, the grain is very attractive with the browns appearing against the lighter wood."

As the walls started up from the rock base, Papa mixed up some sand and water and dirt and Mama and the children helped him push it in between the logs for chinking. It filled the cracks, but Papa wasn't sure the mixture was right for it. He wished he had some lime and that the soil were more like clay. Then it might keep the weather out.

A cool breeze from the northwest one day reminded Mama that the year was getting on. She was proud that Papa had started their cabin, but she was thinking of the winter months to come. She knew that each family could be isolated much of the time if the big snows came. She tended to brood over the loneliness, and here in this place, with its strange inhabitants with ways much different from their own, the uncertainties and, yes, fears. The holidays would come, too, and the women would feel that same desolation that they had known in the old countries when winter came.

Barbara urged John to make a trip to Jackson. "Before winter comes on," she said, "we need more salt. It is good that the friendly Indian has helped you hunt, to make more meat for the coming winter. But more meat in the barrel means more salt to pack it in, so that the hungry mice will not so easily find the meat before we use it all."

"I had thought of that, when we were out hunting. And I suppose I must also get other supplies, enough to last us until Spring."

"Yes — we need the salt, but also sugar and flour and potatoes. And if you can please get me a bolt of bright cloth, I will share it with your sister. We can both make some new clothes for the children.

They are all growing so fast. And some bright gardiner, curtains, will look nice on the little window you are putting in the cabin wall."

So Papa took time to go to Jackson once again. Before he left with the oxen and wagon he talked to Mama in low tones. Maria could hear snatches of what he said. He spoke of keeping enough firewood handy, staying close to the children and not leaving the island unless necessary.

George had to stay home again, of course, because the time had come to resume the lessons. But before Papa left, George managed to ask him to bring some books about horses, if he could. "Different kinds of horses," he said, "but mostly work horses that help the farmers."

Then, with a promise to do his best to fill their orders, Papa was on his way. But his mind struggled with the question of whether he had enough money in his pocket to buy the necessities and have a little left over for the extras. The small bag of coins he still had, after paying for their passage across the ocean and then across the land, and after paying for the oxen and the wagon, had been getting lighter and lighter, each trip he made to Jackson for supplies.

Old News and New Calico

It was October 5 when Papa came back from Jackson with the supplies. The children eagerly helped unload the wagon. They found that Papa had also brought used books for them, old magazines for their mother, and old newspapers for himself to read during the long winter evenings.

Barbara was overjoyed with the brightness of the bolt of red calico with the tiny blue and yellow flowers and even smaller green leaves scattered daintily all over it. She couldn't wait to share it with Betsey Kushman. She asked, "Must we wait until tomorrow, John, or could we go today?"

"One good visit all around would be a good thing before winter comes," Papa agreed. "It is still afternoon. I left Jackson very early this morning so I could be home before evening."

George said, "We can take the wagon, Papa. The oxen are still hitched to it and there is no water over the neck of land."

"Yes, that is true. Just help me give the oxen some hay and water first, so they will be refreshed."

The ride over to the Kushman cabin was a good reminder of the longer ride in the wagon, the same wagon that brought them here earlier when they left the Kushmans in Wisconsin and came on across Minnesota.

That was when Papa bought the oxen and the wagon that brought them the rest of the way to the lakes that looked so good to him. But now the ride was short and they didn't need to bring the featherticks along to cushion the boards behind their backs.

Barbara thought that at the Kushman cabin it would be like a gjenforening, a reunion, when the two families got together. The men and their wives could visit and the children, all cousins, could play together.

As she positioned herself to jump down from the wagon

Betsy asked, "Mama, why are Howie and Willy and Ann our cousins?"

"Because their mother is your father's sister, dear. And that's why you call their parents Aunt Betsey and Uncle Uriah. And you were named for your Aunt Betsey — "

"Only you left the one "e" out of Betsy's name, Mama," Maria interrupted. "But it sounds the same."

The highlight of the day, for Aunt Betsey, was when Barbara brought in the bolt of calico. It made a bright splash of color in the cabin while the two women eagerly unwrapped it from its core so they could divide it. One length held out from nose to fingertips, with one arm out-stretched, was as close to one yard as could be. Once it was measured, it was cut into two lengths. Then each woman folded her half of the total yardage as she began talking excitedly about what she could make from the cloth.

George played with Howie and Willy. They tried to make a string telephone system from tin sirup pails and a ball of string. George thought a telephone would be a great thing to have, if only it worked better. He wondered if the one Robert Hooke had made almost 200 years earlier had really worked. George thought it was one of the more interesting things he had read about in his school books.

Little Betsy played with Cousin Ann. That left Maria wish-ing Etta were there too, instead of over beyond the slough where the Bumgardners and all the Hertwinkles lived. But just then Aunt Betsey asked Maria if she would like to help her with a lunch. Maria's face brightened.

When the platter of biscuits and cold breast of prairie hen was ready, Maria gladly helped pass it around. Then she went out to the well with Willie to get a pail of fresh water. The first well dug on all the land near the lakes had sup-plied the families on the mainland all summer.

When he found out how good the water tasted, John said

to Uriah, "You have done a good thing. You had the courage to dig a well. This vatn, this water, tastes very good."

Uriah said, "I can help you dig one on the island yet, before the ground freezes. Then you will have good water, too. And Barbara will not have to carry all the water from the lake. And you will not have to chop a hole in the ice this winter to get water. It will be much easier to draw it from a well."

George was thinking that it would be exciting to watch the men dig a well and then watch it fill up with water. And Maria already knew how to lower the bucket into the well. She had watched carefully while Willie drew the water she was passing around.

What Papa Read in the Papers

When the cabin was almost ready, Barbara seemed more cheerful and full of energy than ever. For one thing, she felt that it would be much easier to keep the cabin neat, even if some insects could come in where there were little spaces between the logs. And sand and dirt would come in with the firewood and on their own feet, but it would be easier to sweep up. And, anyway, they would not be outdoors as much, once winter came.

She also thought it would be a good thing that their feet would not be constantly damp and almost sticky, as they were when they lived in the dugout. But the lake took care of that, in warm weather. Now they would need a tub to wash their feet in, and to take baths in.

Barbara remembered the cold nights in the dugout, that first winter. She looked forward to moving into the cabin. Though the dugout seemed warm and cozy in mild weather, from early November until the end of March they had all felt the cold that crept in when the weather was more severe.

But there was another reason for Barbara's change of mood. She thought they would all be safer in the cabin. She thought they would be better protected from intruders and strangers — especially Indians.

Late one afternoon in November, the Olesons were finally snug and secure in their new home. It was finished. Papa had found some grey powdery material in Jackson. He said it was called masonry cement. He had also bought a bag of lime. He mixed portions of the two with sand and lake water until the mixture was good and sticky.

George had helped push the soft, sticky mixture into the spaces between the logs on the outside and on the inside, too. Papa said, "The lime in it will turn it white soon. But we will have to do the chinking as a regular fall chore to keep the cold winter winds out and to keep the snow from sifting in."

Betsy thought the walls already looked like layer cake, with lots of frosting between the layers that were the rough logs. "Papa said the lime will turn it white. When it does, it will look like better frosting yet," she said.

Maria's dimple showed when she said to Betsy, "It might look like it, but we will not eat it, will we. We would either crack our teeth or have a mouthful of gritty, sandy stuff to spit out!"

As Betsy laughed at the thought, her smile spread over her whole face. She liked having her sister understand her. They were not only sisters; they were good friends, too.

Mama had made some of the bright calico into curtains. The two panels hung straight down from the top of the square window where she had nailed them up. They were neither ruffled nor full, but they covered the pane and made the cabin look more cheerful. And when they were finished, there was still enough calico left for the other things Barbara wanted to make from it.

George sat by the window in the last minutes of daylight. He was reading about draft horses.With Betsy in her lap, Mama was putting the finishing touches to a hand-sewn dress for Maria.

Maria sat next to her father, who was reading one of the old newspapers he had brought home from Jackson in October. She saw the large print at the top of the paper. It said, "Spirit Lake Massacre Retold" and, in smaller print, something about "Renegade Sioux."

"Papa," she asked, "what are you reading about?"

"Maria, I will tell you what this newspaper story is about. But do not be frightened. It is over. It happened some time ago."

"Yes, Maria," her mother explained. "It happened at

Spirit Lake down in Iowa in March of 1857. That is over two years ago now, before we even left Norway. And since then, our people are more confident that is safe to live in this part of the state. More arrive each year."

"But what happened? What does that word massa...massacre...mean?"

"Not anything pleasant for young ladies to be thinking about at nearly bedtime. But it is better that you know, so you will have the right understanding."

"About that word, Papa?"

"About what happened at Spirit Lake. A few of the Sioux Indians had a very bad leader. He was angry and unhappy and mean. His own people did not like him. He and a few others who went with him killed a number of white settlers at Spirit Lake and Lake Okoboji. Then they ransacked their cabins and burned almost all of them. The paper says they looted them first."

"What is 'looted,' Papa?"

"Looted means they took whatever they wanted from the cabins. It says they also took things they did not want and left them scattered on the ground outside. One of them cut open a family's feathertick and scattered the feathers all over everything, inside and outside, all through the air."

"What happened to the people, Papa?"

"It is a sad story. The article tells us that in just a few days about forty white settlers were killed. Four women were allowed to live, but they were taken away as captives of the Indians. But before the Indians left, they took very young children from their mothers' arms and dashed them against an oak tree near one cabin."

"Is that why you and Mama always want us to stay close by and not wander off out of sight?"

"I do not see any danger to us. Yet...it happened at Spirit Lake and the Okoboji Lakes. But do not fear. The Indians who hunt and fish near us have always been good neighbors. Let us pray that the bad leader does not know we are here, and that the paths he takes will not lead..."

"John," Barbara interrupted gently, "do you not think Maria has heard enough grusom detaljer for one day?"

"That is true, Barbara. Maria...George...Betsy...it is later that I thought. Tomorrow will be another day. Let us hope it will be a glad, a happy one. Good night, dear children."

A Shadow on the Curtains

"Mama," George asked one morning, "when is Thanksgiving? Is it soon?"

"Yes, soon. Very soon. And we will not have lessons on that day. But this morning we will. Now, let me hear you recite those times tables."

George looked up from his book. Thinking it would be fun to be playing out in the snow now that the wind was still and the sun was out, he started with "Two times two is four..."

"George, the two's are too easy. You learned them long ago when you were as young as Betsy is now. Try starting with seven times eight."

"All right, Mama. I'm not sure of them, but I'll try. Seven times eight is fifty-four...no, fifty-six. Seven times nine is...Mama, there's someone outside."

"George...!"

"Honest, Mama. I was looking at the curtains and I saw a shadow. Someone went by the window."

"Papa is outside. It was probably Papa. Now let's get back to the numbers. Seven times nine is...?"

Maria seemed to enjoy her lessons more than George did. There was no holding her back or coaxing her to study. She especially liked to read the books about things that happened to families in Norway in the early times. She was fascinated by the pictures of snowy mountains and fjords, and the tiny farms built on steep, rocky slopes. "It was all so different from our flat prairie here," she often said when she was reading.

When Mama stepped outside for a moment, Maria whispered, "What do you think it was, George? At the window, I mean."

"I couldn't see it because of the curtain. I could only see the shadow. But I think it was a man, tall as the window... maybe an Indian."

"Sh! Mama's coming back in!"

When Papa came in to eat, he exchanged looks with Mama before he greeted the children. As Mama looked directly into his eyes she saw a veiled look that said, "Say nothing now. We will talk about it later." Then he lifted Betsy and tousled her blond curls while she held an old book up to him and begged, "Read it, Papa? Read it?"

"I think the book will wait, if you will. It looks like Mama has food on the table. George and Maria, how did your lessons go this morning?"

Maria answered first. "I read three stories, Papa. I like to read the ones about the old days in our old homeland. Oh, and George was saying his times tables, until he saw a shadow go by the window. Were you out there by the window, Papa?"

"Yes, Papa," Mama echoed, "were you out there? I saw tracks when I looked out but I didn't see you."

"I was outside, Mama. But these poached eggs look good — a real treat. Where did you get fresh eggs?"

"Joanna brought some from their place. They brought a few chickens along when they traveled here from Wisconsin. Now, the hens aren't laying as many eggs, so these truly are a treat. Oh, and they have a cow, too. Joanna promised to send over some butter and milk before Christmas."

"Is everyone ready? Let it wait, George. We'll hear from you later. Fold your hands. Heavenly Father, bless this food; we are thankful for it. Bless our family and friends as we work and play and study. (At the word study George looked up to see if his father was looking at him, but he wasn't.) Bless our neighbors, also the dark ones, and let us be accepting and helpful to each other. Let all our children be safe and secure in their homes in our new land. Amen."

Right after she repeated the "Amen," Maria looked up to see Mama looking at Papa. She wondered what they knew that she didn't know.

She didn't have to wonder very long after they finished eating. During the skrangel, the clatter, of clearing and cleaning the dishes and pans, she heard Papa tell Mama, "Yes, it was an Indian. I went to him when I saw him near the cabin. He rubbed his belly and then he looked out toward the frozen lake and waved his arms toward the woods, and somehow I knew he was saying that the game was scarce and his family was hungry. He looked hungry, too. I could tell he was asking for meat, so we walked to the old dugout where ours is stored. I gave him some venison and he left."

During Papa's prayer before their meal, Barbara had been thinking about how much more secure and comfortable they all were in the cabin. And now that they were in it, the oxen could keep warm in the dugout, with a strong, slender tree trunk stretched across the front of the salt barrel so the oxen couldn't reach it or knock it over. Now, she pictured the Indian going into the dugout with John and seeing just where everything was in there — the oxen, the barrel of salted-down meat, some of John's tools, and a stack of firewood. She said, "I hope they do not come too often, or help themselves again when we are not here."

"We will share what we have, as long as we have food. He was one of those who came and helped us trim off branches and lift the logs into place when we were building the cabin. I heard the others call him by name. It was 'Cante Waste Wicasa.'"*

Barbara whispered the Indian name several times, trying to get used to pronouncing it. Then she asked John, "Do you know what it means?"

"Wilkin told me it means 'Man With Good Heart.' But say no more. Maria is listening."

*(The c is pronounced as ch; the s as sh. So: Chante Washte Wichasha.)

Snowbound Before Christmas

Winter set in to stay after Thanksgiving. Once the ground was cold, the snow stopped melting. When the winds came they piled the loose snow into hard drifts as high as the cabin roof. More snow fell. The strongest winds blew snow through the cracks in the cabin walls, where the chinking was drying out.

More than once Maria tried to wipe the snow off the slab table, but the dirt had blown in with it and the snow melted a little inside, so that the old pieces of woven sack became a sticky, dirty mess.

Maria asked, "Where does this dirt come from, Papa? Isn't the prairie all covered with snow by now?"

"Not every bit of it. The wind blows much of the snow into the grassy patches. But over in the fields, where we broke up the sod, the wind can swoop up the loose dirt from the furrows and ridges. It mixes with the snow and blows on with it."

Mama added, "And when we melt it for washing and bathing, it does not make very clean water."

Betsy was listening. She said, "The snow is prettier where it is clean, Papa. It looks like a snow cake." Her face broke into the widest smile possible. "Oh, Mama, can we make a snow cake? Can we? Please?"

"Today the snow near the cabin is dirty and it is packed hard from the wind. We need fresh, fluffy, clean snow to make a snow cake. Maybe the next time it snows, we can do that, if you will remember to ask then. And maybe Maria would like to help you make the cake."

"I am sure I will remember, Mama. And Maria can help me." Betsy closed her eyes tightly to help herself remember.

The first weeks of winter went by slowly, it seemed to George. He couldn't wait to be over in their field, planting

the wheat. And he hoped for a chance to ride Trader
Wilkin's horses sometime, maybe when Howie's father was
using them, once Spring came to stay.

To Maria, who missed her friend Etta, the winter also
seemed to pass very slowly. But Mama and Papa both listened to their lessons in the mornings, and Maria liked that.
Papa let her read from some of the old newspapers, too.

In the afternoons the children were allowed to play outside if Papa was out cutting wood. George liked stacking the
wood. He said he was making his fort. He didn't mention
the Indians, though. He thought that might scare Betsy.

Well ahead of Christmas Day, Barbara mixed a batch of
flatbrod. It would keep well all through the holiday season,
and it could be baked in the metal box-like oven that she set
on top of the wood-burning stove whenever she wanted to
bake anything.

Barbara asked Maria to
help her mix and shape the
flatbrod. Maria stirred the
graham flour, white flour,
salt and a very small amount
of lard together. Mama
added the boiling water,
and Maria stirred it again.
Then they let it stand until it
was cold before Barbara
added a little more flour,
just enough to make it of a
consistency that could be
rolled out. She said, "It must
be rolled very thin, Maria."

Maria enjoyed the challenge of rolling the dough thin
enough without having it tear apart into pieces. Then
Barbara baked the whole thin, flat sheet on a dark tin pan

that she put on the rack in the oven.

While she helped her mother, Maria forgot all about the Indians and the loneliness that hung over her at times.

A little later, on a calm day in late December, John Hertwinkle walked over the packed drifts to bring the butter and milk Joanna had promised. Barbara thought, It is just in time for making Christmas treats.

Late that afternoon while George romped around on high snowdrifts and jumped from the cabin roof onto the highest ones, Maria and Betsy stayed indoors. Mama gave Betsy some string and a square of cardboard with rows of big holes in it. Betsy sat cross-legged on the feathertick, oblivious to all else. She was absorbed in what she was doing. She was proud that she was learning to sew.

Maria was the one who really was learning to sew. Mama gave her some scraps of the calico that were left, and then showed her how to thread a needle and tie a knot in the end of the thread. Mama let her use real thread.

The first thing that Maria made, which George said he could even recognize, was a doll. Maria had cut two larger scraps of the cloth into the general shape of a doll's body and head. After she sewed them together most of the way around the edges, Mama said, quietly, "Wait a minute, Maria.You can stuff these pieces of worn-out stockings into the doll and it will look more real."

"Oh, yes — and then stitch the edges together the rest of the way around. How nice it will look!"

"For a face, you can sew on buttons for eyes — and pieces of yarn for a mouth, if you unravel a little of your old red sweater."

"Oh, what fun, Mama." Her dimple appeared as she smiled and asked, "Do we have some bright blue buttons, Mama?" Then she spoke very softly, "I will make this one for Betsy, and surprise her with it for Christmas. She is concentrating so hard on her own sewing she will not even know I am making it. And I want to make one for Etta, too, and give it to her the next time I see her, even if I can't give it to her on Christmas!"

While each girl worked at her own kind of sewing, Barbara said, "We will not have a big celebration this year, and we will not go to visit our relatives, because there is so much snow. But we can be glad in our hearts. And we can sing the songs."

"Sing one now, Mama," Betsy begged.

And so Mama began to sing:

> "Du gronne, glitrende tre, god-dag!
> Velkommen du som vi ser sa gjerne
> med jullelys under hjemmets tak
> og hoit i toppen den blanke stjerne!
> Ja den ma skinne, for den skal minne
> oss om var Gud."

When Barbara sang the same song in English, the girls joined in:

> "O green and glittering tree, today
> We welcome you with a song of gladness,
> With toys and candles in grand display,
> Thy beaming star which removes all sadness;
> For ever shining And us reminding
> about our God."

That evening, after the children had fallen asleep, Barbara thought about the doll Maria had just finished. It pleased her to see that her eldest seemed to be content in their new home, and that she was not always thinking only of herself, but also of others. Of Betsy, and of her friend Etta. A friend her own age would be a good thing for Maria as she continued to show signs of womanhood.

Maria Bakes a Snow Cake for Christmas

The next morning — Christmas morning — the children were already excited to see a few small packages stacked on the slab table. Then, when Papa came in from the woodpile, Betsy shouted, "Papa! Papa! Your beard is all white! Is it snowing?"

"No, Betsy," John said quite seriously. "Your Papa has just grown very, very old very fast. See? His hair is all white and his eyelashes and eyebrows and beard are, too." But he couldn't help bursting out laughing a happy, hearty laugh. In spite of the hardships of pioneering, life was good here in their home, and he was glad for any pleasure the children could find in it.

"Oh, Papa," Barbara said, "du plager meg! Such a tease you are! Yes, Betsy, it is snow in Papa's beard. See, he has brought some in with the wood, too."

"Oh, goody, goody, Mama! Maria can help me make a snow cake today!"

"Yes, if it snows enough. Remember, you will need two cups of nice, fresh, fluffy snow for it. It cannot be melted like this that has dripped onto the floor from the wood."

As she mopped up the water from the flat surface of the split logs that formed the cabin floor, Barbara said, "Since today is a holiday, we can do without the lessons for a change. You may open your gifts this morning, and after dinner we can make the snow cake for our Christmas treat."

Papa heard squeals of delight from Betsy and caught the dimple appearing on Maria's cheek. Even George smiled with pleasure and anticipation.

First Maria gave Betsy her calico doll, and then Papa handed out gifts to each child: a book about Belgian horses for George, a set of real sewing cards for Betsy, and a miniature sewing machine "that really sews," Papa said, for Maria. The parents received tight hugs from each child, a gift they

valued more than any object they might have received
under other circumstances. In this new life, new land, new
home, their family meant so much more to them than material possessions did.

Then Mama found the recipe for Snow Cake and
explained to Maria and Betsy that in recipes, the abbrevia-
tion c. meant cup, and a small t. or tsp. meant teaspoon, but
a capital T. alone meant tablespoon.

"But Mama, this recipe doesn't have any big T. in it. Oh, I
can't wait to begin! And it's still snowing! May we make it
now?" Maria asked.

"Right after dinner, Maria, if Papa will get the snow in
then."

Maria studied the recipe. While Mama finished preparing
the dinner, Maria tried to think of something special to put
on the table for their noon meal. She knew the lovely pyra-
mid centerpiece had been left with Bestemor Oleson.
Because it was made of such lightweight, delicate pieces of
wood, it might have broken even if carefully packed
between clothing and bedding in the trunk. And if it were
broken, it would not balance well and turn smoothly as the
small candles burned and created the air currents that kept
its top parts going around and around.

But Maria thought of something else. Leaving the heavy
door open just an inch or two, she stepped outside and
quickly broke a small end branch from a snow-covered tree
near the door. She brought it in and barely had the door
closed before Betsy squealed with delight. "So it is still
snowing!"

Maria shook her head in the affirmative even as she
shook the snow from her hair and from the small branch.
Then she found a large spool of thread and stood the
branch up in its hole so that she and Betsy could hang small
strands of brightly colored yarns on the twigs. Even while

they did that, Maria realized she had left the door open purposely in case any Indians were out there. Then she told herself, They wouldn't come near our cabin on Christmas Day — but she couldn't quite convince herself of that. She saw that Mama was even watching to see that she was safely back inside and had the door closed, before she went on preparing the meal. But at least the small centerpiece made the table and the meal more festive, and Maria was glad she had thought of it.

When they were through eating and the table was cleared, Mama said they could make the cake now.

When Maria was ready, she stirred 1 c. of sugar and 1/3 c. of butter together until what was in the bowl was very smooth and creamy. Then she stirred in 1 tsp. of vanilla.

Into another bowl Mama had measured out 2 tsp. of baking powder and 1/2 tsp. of salt. Betsy mixed these together and stirred in 1 3/4 c. of sifted flour. She could hardly wait until Maria had measured the flour for her.

When Mama said, "I hope this flour is not too heavy," Betsy said, "It doesn't feel very heavy when I stir it." That brought a quick smile on Mama's and Maria's faces.

Maria was ready to put it all together. Mama said the oven was almost ready, so Maria followed Mama's directions to finish the cake. She sifted part of the flour, baking powder and salt mixture into the creamed butter, sugar and vanilla. She stirred it with the strong wooden spoon. Then she let Betsy pour in part of the 1/2 c. of milk. After stirring in more of the dry ingredients, Maria put in the rest of the milk and let Betsy stir it again.

Finally the last of the flour mixture was to be stirred in. Wanting to prolong the pleasure of mixing the cake, Betsy picked up the sifter containing the last part of the flour mixture and gently shook and tapped the sifter so she could watch the flour disappear through the screening.

Suddenly she stopped and asked, "Oh! What is this thing in the sifter?"

It took only a quick look for Barbara to recognize the larva of a grain weevil. She said, "It's just a weevil, Betsy. They get into the flour sometimes, especiallly when it's stored for a while. It won't hurt the cake."

"But I'm glad I just shook the sifter and didn't turn the handle for the last part of the flour. At least, I didn't grind the bug up into the snow cake!"

Maria said, "But you still have to stir the rest of the flour into the batter, Betsy."

While Betsy stirred the batter again, Mama said, "You'd better put in the snow now before it melts. Papa just brought it in while Betsy was stirring."

"All right, Mama. But I want to measure it." Maria carefully dipped the tin cup measure into the pail of snow. Betsy dumped the first cupful into the bowl. Maria stirred it carefully. Mama showed her how to fold it in, under and over and through the middle with the spoon. The second cupful folded in more easily, because the batter was softer now. Maria poured the cake batter into the square pan Mama had greased and floured for her.

Of course, George tore himself away from his book about horses and showed up just in time to argue with Betsy about who got to lick the bowl. Maria settled it diplomatically. She said, "How about you take the spoon, George, and let Betsy have the bowl? That way she can use her fingers to clean the bowl out, and then lick her fingers. They're probably cleaner than yours are."

George, satisfied with that arrangement, overlooked the import of Maria's remark. But he quickly dipped the spoon into the panful of cake batter before Barbara picked up the pan and put it in the hot oven. He was even with his sister now.

Betsy was delighted that there was plenty of snow left in the pail. She played with it for a long time, dipping into it and measuring it and stirring it in the mixing bowl until her hands were cold, her dress was soaked and the snow had all turned to water. George said sarcastically, "If you thought you were making snow pudding, I don't think it's going to be very good. It looks like you put too much water in it."

Betsy started to pout, but just then Mama said, "The real snow cake has been in the oven for thirty minutes. Let's see if it is done." When she tested it with a stiff stem of dried grass she said, "It is done. But because of the snow in it, it is still very moist. Let's let it stand in the oven for just a few more minutes to let the steam out. Maybe just two or three."

When she took the cake out of the oven Mama said, "We must let the cake cool now. But we can make some frosting and have it ready. What is so funny, George?"

"Mama, the cake is a snow cake. You baked it, and now you're going to frost it. Make up your mind!"

"That is funny, George, when words come together like those did — frost the snow cake. But let's do it. The cake is so plain, you'll like it better frosted — or you could say, iced."

The cake was devoured as dessert after supper. All of it. After the last crumbs were gone and the last scrape of frosting was off the plate, Papa asked, "Mama, did you bring the recipe from Norway?"

"No, Papa. But we could have made it there."

"Where did you get it, then?" he asked.

"Aunt Betsey gave it to me when she came over to visit that day. We were thinking about the long winter coming, and she gave me the snow cake recipe. She said, 'I think Maria will want to learn to cook and bake soon.' Then she said, 'My Ann is still much too young, but not Maria. And I think Betsy will want to help.'"

Mama finished, "I tucked the recipe away in the box until today. I knew it would be a long time before the girls could try it."

Before the children went to bed, they sang:

> "Glade jul! Hellige jul!
> Engle daler ned i skjul!"

Then, realizing that the next lines were hard for Betsy to sing in Norwegian, Mama switched to English. They began again:

> "Silent night! Holy night!
> All is calm, all is bright
> Round yon virgin mother and Child!
> Holy Infant, so tender and mild,
> Sleep in heavenly peace,
> Sleep in heavenly peace."

Christmas Day in 1859 had been a fredlig, a peaceful, joyous day for the Oleson family. They did without a real Christmas tree, but Betsy made up for it when she insisted, "We did have a tree. When Papa came in with his beard and hair all snowy this morning, he looked like a tree decorated with tiny, fancy snowflakes. Until they melted!"

George said, "We had two trees, if you call the centerpiece Maria and you made for the table a Christmas tree!"

As they sat in a close circle on the floor and joined hands, Papa brought the day and their modest celebration to a fitting close with a sincere prayer of thanks for the Christ child, God's gift to man, as well as for everything else they had to be thankful for — family, home, food, land, friends and peace. Barbara added to Papa's prayer, "And may all our relatives and neighbors also be well and as happy as we are here in our new home."

George thought of their other near neighbors, the Indians, and hoped they were all friendly and had enough to eat. Maria thought of her friend Etta. She had not had a chance to give her the calico doll she had made for her, but it would not be forgotten about. And Betsy fell asleep hugging her very own new calico doll to her heart.

The Wheat Is Planted

Most of the snow melted by late March. All the families were glad that Spring was near. The wagon-trail road was so packed and firm that it dried off first. Papa was eager to go to Jackson to buy the seed wheat.

One day in the first week of April, he hitched the oxen to the wagon again. Mama gave him her list. He said he just might get a few hens, too, so they could have fresh eggs more often. "That is, if the money stretches somehow to cover all the items."

Before Papa left, he told George, "There is something you can do outside while I am gone. You can take the garden fork and the hoe from the dugout and see if you can dig up the roots out of the garden spot we cleared off for Mama last fall. It will not be a big garden, but it will be a better one after you do that. The roots are tough, like in the field. Work at it a little every day, but keep your eye on the dugout and the cabin, too. If you see any strangers nearby, go to the cabin and tell Mama right away."

George knew that by strangers Papa meant Indians. But he thought it would be more fun to watch for arrowheads, when he dug those roots out, than to watch for Indians.

While Papa was gone, though, George did see some Indians. It was on the second day. He saw at least seven of them, but by the way the slough grass moved, he thought maybe more than seven could be hiding in it. None of them was Cante Waste Wicasa — at least, none of those he could see clearly.

One was an older man; the rest appeared to be younger. All of them had painted lines and designs on much of their copper-colored skin so that they looked very strange, and some of them wore a few feathers in their headdresses. George just stood there on the garden spot and stared at them. He was fascinated by how colorful they were, and how close. But they moved on, through the edge of the slough and eastward along Jack Creek, George guessed, and on toward Heron Lake and the Des Moines River. George kept this information to himself until Papa came home, because Betsy was always around when he could have told Mama about it, so he didn't have a chance.

After Papa came home from Jackson, the weather was mild and calm. It began to feel like Spring. There was suddenly much outdoor work to be done, and each one went about it eagerly.

While George helped Papa build a pen for the new chickens, he told Papa about the Indians he had seen. Since they had moved on without causing any problems, Papa seemed to forget about them, at least for now. His mind was on the field work that had to be finished as soon as possible.

Betsy and Maria helped Mama put away the fresh supplies. Papa put the cloth sack of seed wheat in the cabin to keep it dry. He said, "It should not germinate before it is planted in warm soil in the field."

Before the seed could be planted, however, Papa went to the field almost every day. He hitched the oxen to the plow, but he attached a different part to its wooden beam. This one he had just bought in Jackson looked more like a heavy, coarse rake. He called it a drag. He said its iron teeth would break up the soil into even smaller particles now that the melting snow and early spring rains and sunshine had mellowed it.

When Papa finished going through the field with the drag, he told George, "I am glad I found the drag for sale at Jackson. Its owner had given up on farming and had gone back East, so the storekeeper gave me a good price for it. And it worked well. Now the field is ready for the seed."

George watched Papa fill a can from the bag. Then he attached the handle to the large container he had filled with

seed. They walked to the field
together, Papa carrying two heavy
pails filled with more seed from
the bag. He let George carry the
Cyclone seeder, with a warning
not to spill the seed. "And do not
turn the handle until I tell you."

Once in the field, Papa took over. He carried the seeder
by a strap over his shoulders, steadying it with one hand
while with the other he turned the handle. The seed scattered in a circle around Papa as he walked back and forth
across the field.

It seemed that all the men were happy to be at their
spring work. Twice Papa and George "halloed" loudly at
Uncle Uriah and the two older Hertwinkle boys and Uncle
Thomas, and they all shouted back. They were helping Uncle
Uriah get his field ready to plant. George knew that when it
was seeded, Uncle Uriah would help William Hertwinkle
and his sons and Uncle John, Monnie's father. Thomas was-
n't married, so he helped everybody wherever he could find
farm work to do. He didn't have a place of his own yet.

George asked, "Papa, will we help someone else when
our field is all planted?"

"Son, when someone asks for help, we will be glad to
help. But we only have one small field. We can take care of
it ourselves. Then while we wait for the wheat to sprout and
grow, we can help Mama with her garden. After that, we can
cut and stack firewood. And catching fresh fish takes some
time, too. We do not lack for work on our own land."

George had a feeling that in spite of his father's usual
calm, he might be feeling a little unsureness, perhaps
almost fear. He thought it might have something to do with
the Indians who were here before them and were still here.

When George remembered about those Indians who had

passed their place while Papa was gone, he knew the reason. George had been curious and fascinated, almost awed by their appearance that day. But now he feared what might have happened if they were not friendly Indians. Now he knew that he should have told his mother about them right away. And he should have told his father in more detail as soon as he had come home. Perhaps there was good reason to fear them. George knew that his father was always on the alert and seemed glad to have plenty of work to keep him busy on his own land.

Papa Learns About the Census

With the help of mild, sunny days and several gentle rain showers, the wheat germinated and emerged. Even Barbara and the girls enjoyed walking together to the mainland to see the blades standing green against the dark soil. Here and there they could still see some dark patches of ground, where Papa said the seeder didn't scatter the seed evenly. Before long, they could all see the patch of green, even from their island.

"Now it is up to the good Lord and the weather He sends us," John said. He was looking forward to harvesting that first crop of grain. If it was not destroyed by a natural disaster, such as drought or hail or fire, and if there was enough grain harvested, he could go to Jackson to trade it for supplies instead of using his last silver dollars. He knew that a portion of the grain would have to be kept at home for seed for the next season, but if Jackson had a molle, a mill, by the next fall, some of their very own wheat could be ground into flour there.

John thought that was a real possibility. Since his family and friends had settled here, the area was beginning to fill up fast. As more people came and the settlements grew, stores, hotels and mills appeared in the towns.

John Oleson hoped and prayed that no disaster would overtake his family or their neighbors. But he also knew that some of the Indians were not as friendly as those who camped around the slough and fished in the lakes in the summer. Every time he saw a canoe on the lake, he hoped it was one of their friendly Indians. He hoped they were finding enough to eat.

One day in the first part of the summer Barbara said to John, "I wonder how we would feel if our land and our sources of food like the wild game were taken from us by the Indians, as we have taken theirs."

Papa said, "I think I know. And here we are, along with others, so eager to claim land for a new home, a new beginning, that we did not even wait for all of the Indians to leave. We moved right in on them and among them. But, so far, we can trust our Indian friends here. They have been helpful."

That summer, Papa had to make an extra trip to Jackson. Mama needed flour and salt again. Papa asked at the store if any papers or letters had come for them. While he was there, he heard the person who took care of the mail speak about the folketelling, the census, that was being taken in some nearby counties.

"What is it all about?" John asked a man at the general store.

"The federal government is taking a census. That means a count of the people in the area. They know that many have come west and they want to know who is here, now that Minnesota is a state of the United States."

"So will someone also come to Graham Lakes? There are several families there, with thirty-some people in all. They should be included."

"I will tell Elias. When he finishes the Jackson County listing, he can ride his horse to your lakes and add your group of settlers to the census."

"What will he want to know?"

"The main information required will be your names, ages, what kind of work you do, and where you were born. The forms say name, age, occupation and birthplace at the top."

"I will remember that, and we will be ready when he comes to our homes. You call him Elias?"

"Yes. His name is Elias D. Bruner. He is an assistant marshal. Do you have a county seat or a name for your county?"

"The Graham Lakes are in Nobles County. I read in the papers that the county was designated in 1857, but then there was a delay in getting the government organized. I believe there will soon be more settlers there, as soon as the railroad comes, and the whole county will be thriving. Towns will be organized. There has been some talk of Gretchtown as the county seat, but there is no such town as yet.

"I thank you for explaining to me about the census. Now I must start home and tell my friends about it."

A sod house at Pioneer Village in Worthington, Minnesota

The Census Is Taken

One day in the middle of July George saw a man riding
toward the island on a large roan horse. He carried a pack
different from Trader Wilkin's saddlebags. George was
about to hail him and try to wrangle a ride on the horse
when Papa came around the cabin from over by the dugout.

"Hallo!" and "Howdo!" were followed by an exchange of
names, and John Oleson asked Elias Bruner how the cen-
sus-taking went at Jackson.

"Jackson County has 181 people," Elias said. "And now, I
am ready to take the census for Nobles County."

He took a black bound record book, a pen and a small,
square bottle of ink from his flat leather pouch. John told
Elias the names and ages of the members of his family and
their place of birth. Then he said, "I am a farmer, though it
is slow work. And we have relatives here. The Kushmans
also came from Norway when we did, but they stopped over
in Wisconsin when it was time for their Ann to be born.
Now they are also here, and Ann is already two."

When he had finished recording the information about
the Oleson family, Elias closed his book and put his pen and
the ink bottle away. He said, "I thank you kindly, but I must
get the information directly from each household. You can
help, though, by telling me where each family lives and how
I can best reach their places."

And so the federal census of 1860, taken on July 16 in the
Graham Lakes area in the northeast corner of Nobles
County, Minnesota, was added to the Jackson County census as a last page and signed, "Elias D. Bruner, July 16,
1860."

As the men gathered to help each other with their work
and the women and children now and then visited back and
forth before the cold weather set in, one topic of conversation was the census and how it affected them. John com-

mented, "We will no doubt have to do something about a skole, a school, soon. Mr. Bruner noted that, all together, we have nine children between the ages of five and sixteen. When I told him we were all teaching our children at home, he said we should think about having a school with a qualified teacher."

Once when they were talking about the need for a school, Maria asked, "Oh, Papa, could we start a school on the island? Then I could see Etta almost every day, and Howie and Willie could come, and Etta's sister Wilmy."

"And Marie and William Hertwinkle," Papa added. "They are not too old to learn more from lessons."

"Trapper Thomas Marks is the only grownup here that has not learned to read or write. Perhaps he would also like to attend," Mama said.

A New Excitement in the Settlement

When fall came, all the settlers agreed that a school
would be good. Barbara could be the laererine, the teacher,
because she had no small children. Hers were all old
enough to go to school. Julia Hertwinkle promised to help
because her three were the oldest of all the children in the
settlement. When her husband needed help their oldest son
Thomas, who was eighteen, could stay home and help him.

There was a new excitement in the settlement that fall.
After the grain was harvested the men were tired, but they
were happy. Their first attempt to raise grain in the new
land was a success. No natural disasters had come to
destroy the fields. Their talk was jovial as were the men
when they planned to choose and mark the trees that would
become logs for the walls of the school. The trees to be
marked could not be too old, nor too young. They must be
straight as an arrow, and could not have too many branches
down low on the trunk.

But the cold weather and heavy snow came early that
year and the men were in no hurry. "Spring is a better time
for building a log cabin," they said.

And so they waited while the winter of 1860-1861 went
by.

When Barbara mentioned the school one night at the
supper table, John said, "Vaar, Spring, is also the time for
planting the grain again." And when Spring came, that's
what the men did.

And so, much of the year passed. When the field work
was finished in early October and all families had an ample
supply of firewood, Barbara remarked, "And now the children are all a year older. Maria is twelve. George is nine.
And Betsy is seven already. And still no school."

That kind of talk on the part of each of the women goad-
ed their men to action.

One day Papa said to Uriah, "Before the coldest months come, let us build a cabin for a school. Then next Spring, when the snow and winter winds let up, we can go ahead with our field work and planting, but the children can go to school. They will not have to wait again, for another year."

The word spread. The men worked together to begin their school. By November three walls of a new cabin stood to one side, near the neck of the island but a little farther up the gentle slope. There was no fourth wall and no roof before the winter storms struck.

It turned out to be such a severe winter that the other children could not have walked to the island to attend the school, even if it had been completed. They would have to wait for better weather and the completion of the project.

One day that winter, when everyone seemed to be tired of being indoors and Maria was feeling lonesome for her friend Etta, she opened the trunk that stood in the corner of their cabin now. Reaching down beneath the folds of clothing, she felt around until she found what she was looking for. She took out the three birthday plates.

Betsy, never away from her sister's side for very long at a time, said,"Oh, Maria, let me see them again. I didn't see them for such a long time, I almost forgot we had them."

Barbara said, "Those birthday plates are something I

hope we will never have to part with. They are meant as a reminder to each of you of your full names and birthdates. Having one made and rosemaled for each child is a family custom for many of our people."

As Maria handed one to Betsy she said, "This one is yours, Betsy."

"I see my name. What else does it say?"

"This line says, 'Betsy Julia Oleson.' The second line says, 'daughter of John and Barbara Oleson,' and the last line gives your birth date, 'born April 6, 1854.'"

"Read yours to me, too, Maria. Does it say, 'Maria Anna Oleson,' and then Papa and Mama's names, too?"

"Yes — and then my birth date, 'May 5, 1849.'"

George looked up then and went over to the girls to say, "I know what the other one says. You don't have to read it to me. It's mine, and it says, 'George William Oleson, son of John and Barbara Oleson, born March 4, 1852.'"

Maria noticed the extra emphasis George put on the word "son."

The rest of that winter passed and Spring came again. As the men met each other on their land, checking on the conditions of the soil, there was more talk about finishing the school. It was often interrupted by talk about their dark-skinned neighbors. It seemed that there was more anger among them than before because they had not received the promised payments from the government and because it was so hard for them to find food during the severe winter just past. Many were on the verge of starvation.

Uncle Thomas Hertwinkle was the first one to travel to Jackson that spring. He brought back word that a band of Sioux Indians was believed to be on the warpath, led by a renegade chief that the other Indians didn't trust. Uncle Thomas had been warned to be on the lookout for them on his way home. It was thought that they were camped not far from the Graham Lakes area, possibly at one of the other lakes nearby. But Uncle Thomas saw nothing of any Indian camp between Jackson and the Graham Lakes, and so no one seemed to be very worried about it.

As a matter of fact, when the storekeeper in Jackson warned Uncle Thomas, he had in mind something that George Wilkin had said the last time he had been in the store. Wilkin had said, "One Indian called Cante Waste Wicasa has been helpful to the settlers at Graham Lakes. That has been a good thing, for the settlers. He and his brothers showed them how to find meat here and helped them later when they were ready to build their cabins. That friendship has also been a good thing for Cante Waste Wicasa and his brothers, because Oleson and Kushman and some of the other whites were willing to share their venison when the wild game became scarce and the Indians were hungry.

"But, in another way, that friendship has not been a good thing."

The storekeeper had asked, "What do you mean, Wilkin? What is the problem?"

Wilkin told him then about the conflict brewing between the friendly Indians and the others. He said, "From all my experience dealing with them as a trader, I have learned that the conferences the Indians hold around their camp-fires are very important to them in every way. But these few friendly Indians have been ostracized by their warlike brothers who refuse to smoke the peacepipe with them at the counsel fires, because they feel differently about the white settlers who have been allowed by the government of the United States to move in here and take over the land and the sources of food that have always belonged to the Indians. They are angry about that, and they are angry with Cante Waste Wicasa and his blood brothers for not agreeing with them."

But the storekeeper had not told Uncle Thomas the whole story, and Wilkin had not yet returned to Graham Lakes to tell the men in the settlement about the conflicts.

Papa and George Get the Message

A few weeks after Thomas Hertwinkle's return from
Jackson, Cante Waste Wicasa came to the island. He seemed
to want to tell John something, but the two could not suc-
cessfully communicate with words. By Man With Good
Heart's actions and the direction he looked with his dark
eyes, John thought maybe he was saying something about
the school walls.

But what was he saying? Finish building it? Tear it down?
Let him live in it? John wished he had learned the language
of the Dakotas, now that he and his family were living so
close to some of them.

Suddenly John became very attentive. He had to watch
Man With Good Heart's motions and his facial expressions
very closely to try to understand him. Man With Good Heart
was motioning to the neck of land that provided the most
direct access to the island. The partially built cabin that was
to become the school stood approximately the width of two
large spruce trees from the approach. Papa knew that the
approach had been kept clear so that he could still go from
the island to the field and back with the oxen and plow or
drag, or go with the wagon to Jackson or to other parts of
the settlement. And the other settlers could also still come
to the island.

Now, all the while beckoning John to follow, Man With
Good Heart walked ahead of John to the building site.
There he pointed to the log walls and made a pushing
motion with his head, arms and shoulders, as if pushing the
unfinished log structure toward the neck of land. After that
motion, he folded his arms across his chest, and his face
took on a very serious expression. He also nodded his head
emphatically several times, his set lips suggesting determi-
nation.

George, watching from near their cabin, was curious

about Man With Good Heart's motions. He came slowly to where the two men stood. Watching the Indian's face and gestures carefully, George made gestures of his own — toward the partially built school and toward what remained of his own "fort." When the Indian repeated his own first gestures and nodded his head again, George said, "Papa, I think he is telling us to move the cabin walls closer to the neck of land there and make us a barricade, like my fort I built with the firewood last year. I saw him sitting on a stump behind it one day, looking at it. Then when he saw me look up, he left."

Man With Good Heart started to walk away, as if now he had been understood. But after a few steps toward the mainland, he paused. Facing the sun, he raised his arms to it. Then, bowing his head, he stood still for a moment, as if invoking the sun to watch over them all, or perhaps over their land. Only he knew.

George asked, "Papa, why do you think he did that just now?"

John answered, "Somewhere I read or heard that, to the Indians, the sun is sacred. They see it as the source of all life. Perhaps he was praying."

While George seemed to be pondering that, Papa resumed an earlier conversation that had started when they were building the pen for the hens. Now Papa was reminded of what George had told him that day. He asked, "And you didn't tell me about Man With Good Heart watching you?"

"I forgot, Papa. I didn't mean to. It was when I was digging the roots out of the garden, and I was watching for arrowheads, too. Some of the men and boys have been finding them. They think the Indians used them earlier, when they hunted on this land. And I did find some."

"But you saw an Indian right here?"

"Yes. This one. He was looking at my fort and watching me. But then he walked away. I put the arrowheads down in the crawl space. I didn't have any way to use them."

"And do you have anything else to tell me now, about the Indians?"

"Well, that other day, when you were gone to Jackson the last time, I saw seven or eight other Indians. One older man walked ahead of the others. They had on a lot of red paint and wore some feathers, but hardly any clothes."

"Why didn't you tell Mama this right away, when it happened?"

"I wanted to, but you said not to scare Betsy, and she was always there beside Mama and Maria every time I thought of it. Anyway, I told you that they moved on, away from here."

"You should have told Mama so she could be ready and watchful..."

"Ready, Papa? For what? More visitors?"

"Never mind that now. Let us go and tell Mama where we are going. Then you may go with me to the other cabins, and we will warn the others. You can tell the men what you saw, and we will tell them what we think Man With Good Heart was telling us today."

A Decision Is Made

Papa and George left a few minutes later to warn the Kushman and the Eavens families. From there they went to the home of George and Ann Bumgardner, Etta's parents. Though they were beginning to understand and speak a little English, an urgent message given briefly was not easy for them to grasp. Etta, however, understood what they were saying and she made sure her parents also understood. They, in turn, would pass the word on to William Hertwinkle, if he was home; otherwise, to his wife Julia, who would see that Uncle John and Uncle Thomas also heard about it.

The three trappers were not yet back from selling their last catch of hides, and the McFarlane brothers were in Webster City, Iowa, hoping to purchase a team of horses. No one seemed to know where Trader Wilkin had gone. "Business with the Indians, perhaps," someone said, and then changed the subject.

George Evert and Henry Hanson, also traders, were not in their shanties. No one had any idea where they were. They had both come from a long ways away — George from Maine and Henry from Tennessee — and now their shanties looked almost deserted. Not long after the time of the census taking there had been some talk of trouble brewing in the South over the slavery question. Some thought Evert and Hanson might have volunteered as soldiers. Others thought there might be as much need for soldiers right here, before long, if trouble with the unfriendly Indians developed.

After the word was spread to each household, the men and older boys gathered at the schoolhouse site. It wasn't long before they had made a decision. They would make a barricade, a little like George's fort, but much sturdier and larger.

Some of the men were surprised to see an Indian also

appear, but George and John knew it was Man With Good Heart. He worked hard, right along with the others, but he worked quietly and no one questioned his motives.

The three walls had to be unstacked at the two corners and restacked at the location that would offer the most protection if the island were approached by land. That took up most of the rest of the week.

Another day, when the men and boys all came back, they stacked the logs for the fourth wall. As they did, the boys pulled branches from the brush pile and pushed them into the larger spaces left by the unevenness of the logs. The roof was made by laying branches across each corner, with a few longer and stronger branches across the middle of the space. They were put on rather hurriedly, so the roof would offer only a little protection, but there was no time for a more complete roof now. Chinking the walls and adding earth and bundles of grass to the roof would have to wait until there was more time. It was already summer. The grain was growing in their fields.

Rumors Lead to Action

George understood that the barricade was needed to protect them all from the bad Indians, if they came around. He had heard some of the men talking as they worked. They spoke of what the minister from Norway said when he came to hold services. He told the men and women how it was at Spirit Lake and at Springfield in 1857. He said he thought that might happen again, here.

"When the time is right," Reverend Baker told them, "it will happen to other white people. Other Indians or maybe some of the same ones will attack. They do not like having their land and their freedom taken from them. They will be brutal in their treatment of the white settlers. In their anger they may steal your guns, take your clothing and food, and burn your homes."

George shuddered when he heard the men talking about what else the minister had told them: "Your women and children may be killed or taken captive. Protect yourselves the best you can, or leave before it happens. If you leave, go as far as you can from here, to where there are many more people and you will have the help of soldiers and government forts, and more guns and ammunition."

But no one wanted to leave. Their whole lives were centered here, now. Unless, someone suggested, that was why George Evert and Henry Hanson, who had no families with them, were gone already. Perhaps they had been warned earlier and had left on their own, without coming back to the settlement first? Two men traveling alone could be less easily detected. Had they gone to join their families? Or had they gone to join the soldiers at the fort farther to the north?

During the next few weeks, feelings of uncertainty and insecurity worked through the settlement. The warnings and the pastor's advice left them wondering if they were safe in their scattered homes. Some felt it best to leave for Ft. Ridgely, where the soldiers had gone when they abandoned Fort Dodge. "But that is a long way from here," John said. "And we may only be asking for trouble. It is possible that the 'Unfriendlies' have already started out to the northeast toward Ft. Ridgely or New Ulm."

Uriah reminded them, "And the pastor said there is no stockade around the Ft. Ridgely site."

Uncle Thomas Hertwinkle said, "When I went to Jackson last Spring, I was told that at Belmont, a short distance north of Jackson, the settlers were feeling insecure already in the fall of 1860."

Uriah asked him, "What did they do?"

"They organized a company of home guards. The State of Minnesota furnished arms, and the guards drilled every week."

Each man volunteered any information he thought relevant to the situation. Still, it was very hard to make a decision as to whether to stay or leave. Some said, "But we don't know how much time we have before we might be attacked. Perhaps we will be forced to leave before the harvest."

Another said, "That would be too bad, when our fields offer the prospect of a good crop this season. I would certainly not like to..."

Someone interrupted him, "When troops were organized for the Civil War, many able young men enlisted. They became part of a regiment of volunteers from Minnesota. That left both the new Belmont area and the older Jackson area less protected."

Another man said, "I heard that at one Norwegian settlement east of us, where a group of Indians planned to attack, they tired of shooting at blank walls where the people had gathered to resist them. Not knowing how many defenders were assembled there, or how many guns or how much ammunition they had, the Indians actually left rather than chance being defeated."

After several similar discussions, with each one telling what he had heard, the adults agreed: If they stayed together within the barricade they had a better chance than along the way on the open prairie. And now that it was completed, although hurriedly, the barricade might as well be used. They thought that at least they would be better protected there than if they remained scattered at their individual homes.

John said, "Then let us not wait any longer." The others agreed with him that no time should be wasted.

They decided to gather their guns and ammunition and any other weapons they had, in case it became necessary to defend themselves. And so, as soon as they were ready, each family appeared at the barricade. The women brought food and what little clothing and bedding they could carry and brought their children with them. The younger children of school age thought it was for lessons. Maria and George had both heard enough of the adults' talking and planning to know what to expect.

Prayers and Promises

By evening of the next day all the white people presently within the settlement were gathered in the barricade. The men gave orders to their own families to stay inside. They were very serious about it; their orders were to be obeyed at once. It had much to do with what Reverend Baker had told the men earlier, and with what Uncle Thomas had told them when he returned from Jackson.

George found it hard to sleep that night. He was too excited.

Maria was tired, but in another way. She was growing so fast! Mama and Papa treated her like a young lady now, so she had to be polite and ladylike and not be running about like a child. That was hard for her, and she had a lot to think about. Her body was changing, and Mama had told her she would very soon be a woman.

Betsy and Cousin Ann slept well, cuddled comfortably against Maria, with coats and quilts spread over them.

During the night Barbara and Aunt Betsey talked for a long time. They spoke very quietly, but because they sat near her and because Maria was not really asleep, she could hear what they were saying. They were planning what they would do in case of an attack.

Barbara said, "I almost wish we were in our own cabin. Then, if the Indians came near, we could hide down in the crawl space until they left again. We would be crowded down there, but..."

Maria heard Aunt Betsey ask, "But isn't there a way to get into it from the outside? Maybe they would find you, after all."

"Well, but if they came into the cabin when we were down there, then maybe we could get out that way and run from them."

Aunt Betsey said, "When I think of those children swung

time and again against the tree, and those four women so rudely dragged away by the Indians, I shudder to think what could happen to our dear children and to us."

Maria heard her own mother say, "I know John would give his life to defend his family. And the children must be saved at all cost. Are you willing to suffer in their place, if that becomes necessary?"

Aunt Betsey and Mama then made a promise to each other that, if it meant saving their children, each would give herself up to the Indians.

Aunt Betsey said, "Oh but Barbara, that could be so horrible. Promise that if we are taken, you will stay with me and bolster my courage."

Just as Barbara said, "I promise, but I pray that won't happen," the men on watch exchanged places with those who had been resting. Papa sat down next to Barbara and asked her what the promise was all about. After Barbara explained, Papa said, "We both love our children very much. Each one is dear to us in a special way. But what frightens me most is the chance that Maria might be taken by some young brave, to be his property, to do with as he wishes...to be his woman, his slave...you have heard of their ways. She is attractive, but so young, and hardly a mature woman."

Maria, finding it hard to get to sleep after hearing Barbara and Aunt Betsey's conversation, was still awake. She wanted to get up and move to the safety of her parents' arms, but Ann and Betsy were asleep beside her. When she heard her parents pray together for the safety of their own family and of all the others, her lips moved to pray with them. Aunt Betsey also prayed, silently. She felt that was all she could do to help.

It was very quiet in the barricade then. During the rest of the night the men kept watch, one shift gladly giving over to another for several hours at a time.

Friendship Wins

At the first line of light on the horizon, Papa stood straighter. He strained to see to the far expanse of prairie that had not yet been broken, out beyond their small fields. He thought he saw movement that broke the rhythm of the tall grass swaying and bending in a gentle morning breeze.

John had only the old musket that had been his father's, but he had cleaned it and he held it ready to use if it became necessary. At his whispered urging, the men who were resting and the older boys joined the shift on watch. George stood next to Papa, and the other boys took their places next to their fathers. George's cousins were only eight and seven, but they stood next to Uriah.

All of them peered out through the unchinked spaces between the logs that formed the walls. They watched for any unusual movement. George found himself wondering if the other boys were just a little afraid.

Before long, their fears were confirmed. A line of seven or eight mounted and boldly painted Indians approached the island from the direction of the fields. George recognized one of Trader Wilkin's horses among those the painted Indians were riding. He wondered if Wilkin had traded it, or if they had just taken it from him. He knew that Wilkin hadn't been at the settlement for many months.

Before they reached the island, a single Indian walked toward the others from the direction of the slough. He stood his ground near the neck of the island without crossing it. George could see between the logs that it was Man With Good Heart. He was not mounted, and he was not painted like the others.

Maria got up and started over toward George to see what was so interesting. Barbara pulled her back and held her and Betsy close. Aunt Betsey motioned to Uriah to send Howie and Willie back to where she sat holding Ann.

Man With Good Heart was talking with the other Indians. At the same time, he appeared to be letting the white men know what he was saying. Although he still had no way to communicate in words, he hoped they would understand his motions that accompanied his words to the war party.

As he spoke, Man With Good Heart also motioned wide with his arms in a gathering motion. Then he beat on his side many times. It was the side where his knife hung in its sheath. Next he beat on his chest with his fists, and extended his arms in front of his face as if taking aim, but beat his side again many times. All the while, he spoke to the red men in the language of their people. His next motion was the same he had used when he met with John and told him to move the school walls closer to the edge of the island. But now he was motioning away from the island and speaking excitedly and emphatically at the same time. George thought he must be telling the other Indians to ride far, far away. John and George were not surprised at his next gesture. He faced the rising sun and raised his arms to it, then bowed his head, seemingly in humility.

How strange it seemed. Yet from the few observations Papa had made and from all he had heard from others, he believed he understood. Speaking as quietly as he could, he told the men, "I think our friend is telling the others that we are armed and will defend ourselves. Let's try pushing the ends of all the guns into the spaces between the logs."

John turned toward his wife and said, "Barbara, ask the women to give us anything they can find in their belongings — anything that even looks like a weapon of any kind. The Indians might believe we are well armed and can defeat them, as has happened at another place."

The women looked through their hurriedly gathered belongings for objects that when put through the cracks in the cabin walls, would look at least a little like weapons.

Aunt Betsey found her large wooden crochet hook. Ann Bumgardner offered her husband's fishing knife. Wondering how effective Papa's plan could be, they handed the men whatever they thought might help.

But it was not necessary to use any of the weapons. In a short while, the mounted war party turned their horses and rode off, out of sight, as fast as their horses would go, as if they were the ones who were in danger. Man With Good Heart stood behind a stout hackberry tree until the others were all out of sight and he could no longer hear the thunder of their horses' hoofs as they rode on. Then he also left, walking very slowly in the opposite direction.

John and Uriah cautiously left the barricade and the island, hoping to catch up with their friend. George moved swiftly and quietly and caught up with his father and uncle over near the slough.

John Oleson said, "My son, I believe you understand our friend very well, and I am proud that you are not afraid to come with us to thank him for what he has done for us."

Uncle Uriah said, "I hope my own sons will follow your example when they are a little older."

Startled by their voices when they spoke to George, Man With Good Heart turned to face them. He took a few steps toward them. For a brief but very touching moment, John extended his arms toward Man With Good Heart and embraced his good friend warmly. Man With Good Heart returned the white man's embrace. Each saw in the eyes of the other a mutual respect and acceptance.

When John stepped back and placed his right hand above his heart in a gesture of humble gratitude, Man With Good Heart repeated his earlier gesture of facing the rising sun and raising his arms to it. Then he bowed his head for a moment and, when he looked up, he saw that George was repeating that gesture, as if he were one of them. Man With

Good Heart then placed his right hand above his own heart, just as John had done, and looked deeply into George's eyes for a moment before he turned from them and walked on alone in the direction he had started, away from the island, the barricade, and the site of the near confrontation.

Loneliness Is Mutual

When John, Uriah, and George came back to the barricade, everyone was talking at once. Someone asked, "What should we do now?" Others said, "We must think of the good of all," or "We do not want to leave our new homes, but maybe it is best, for now, that we do." Another one said, "Yes. Then when the trouble is settled, we can hope to come back and go on with our lives here."

Some of the families were ready to go back to their own cabins to prepare a meal and to rest, but John and Uriah urged them to wait a little longer until they were quite sure the war party would not return.

A few hours into the afternoon, Man With Good Heart returned, along with Trader Wilkin. All the men were surprised. They had not seen Wilkin for several months.

First, Wilkin explained, "The war party came with the intention of wiping out Man With Good Heart's friends. They were very angry with him because he would not join them in their attacks, so they rejected him and his red brothers that also helped build your cabins. Now they plan to kill Man With Good Heart as well as his white friends that he has been helping."

John asked, "Then why did he come back with you? Surely he realizes the danger."

Wilkin said, "Man With Good Heart came with me to be sure you would be sufficiently warned of the danger you are in. The war party has fled, for now. They have gone into camp at North Heron Lake almost directly east of our lakes here. But before they leave the area they plan to come back here to destroy the whole settlement — every cabin and the barricade and everyone in it."

While Man With Good Heart waited patiently, but watchfully, Wilkin told them all about Karl Zierke, whom everyone called Dutch Charley. He told them that Dutch Charley was the trapper who had come in the winter of 1857 to trap along the tributaries of the Big Cottonwood River. He lived in a dugout that winter and, when Spring came, he left to sell his furs. In 1858 he returned, settling as a squatter in the southeast quarter of section 25 in Ann Township of Cottonwood County, much as the Graham Lakes people had settled here in Nobles County.

It was when Wilkin told them what had happened to Dutch Charley just recently, in this very month, that the Graham Lakes settlers became most frightened.

Wilkin said, "Dutch Charley's family — his woman and her three children, as well as the two children they had together — lived in a cabin almost on the New Ulm-Sioux Falls Trail that passed just south of it. There, they also had oxen, milk cows, cattle and hogs.

"After the first attacks on New Ulm," Wilkin went on, "a German from New Ulm was fleeing along that trail. The German stopped to warn Dutch Charley, as did one of the settlers from Shetek at almost the same moment. After the attack on the settlement at Lake Shetek on August 20, that one settler who escaped outran the Indians and went by way of Dutch Charley's to give the alarm."

While Wilkin paused a moment, several of the Graham Lakes settlers spoke out in alarm. But Wilkin continued, "The Zierkes left immediately by ox team and wagon. Near New Ulm, Dutch Charley left his family and went into the timber to find something for them all to eat. While he was gone, a party of Indians dressed for war appeared. They took Mrs. Zierke and the children as well as the oxen and the wagon."

Wilkin stayed in the barricade with the others from the settlement, but Man With Good Heart left the island and walked slowly back toward the slough.

Having heard all that Wilkin had told them, and having

seen the look of utter despair in ManWith Good Heart's eyes, the Graham Lakes settlers agreed late that afternoon that it would be best for all concerned if they left. "Before the war party returns," John urged them, "or it may be too late to escape."

Before sunrise the next morning, when Man With Good Heart returned cautiously to the settlement, his friends were nowhere to be seen. Their oxen and wagons were gone, but it appeared to him that their cabins and dugouts had not been disturbed, so he thought they must have left by their own will.

He walked on toward the island. He found the log "school," still unchinked, still standing on the narrow neck of land. It had not been disturbed by the Unfriendlies, now his enemies. Wagon wheels had made a trail through the grass and around one end of the barricade. Shallow, quiet water filled the wheel ruts and deep hoofprints of oxen next to the approach and escape point of the island.

Inside the barricade, he found no food, no blankets, no clothing, no weapons. Only one thing remained. At first it looked like a bright scrap of cloth. It turned out to be a stuffed doll made from red calico. It had bright blue button eyes and a red yarn mouth. He picked it up from where it lay in one corner as if its owner had been hurried outside and was forced to leave her treasured friend behind.

He walked beyond the barricade and on toward the abandoned island cabin he had helped build. Standing in the doorway, he looked inside. For the first time he realized somewhat how the Oleson family had lived here, and how sad they must be to leave it and many of their belongings.

He hugged the stuffed calico doll to his chest before he placed it on the slab table. He knew he would not see the Olesons again, but he knew the doll belonged to the girls —

to dear little Betsy who would miss it now, and to lovely Maria with the long, dark hair and the bright blue eyes, who had lovingly created it for her sister.

As Man With Good Heart turned and once again walked slowly away toward the slough, a tear slipped down his cheek. He didn't try to track his friends. He felt that he had done all he could to help them. Now he could only hope they would reach a safe place, a place where they could make another new beginning.

Afterword

Today, the Dakota War and the U.S.-Dakota Conflict are preferred names for what has long been referred to as the Sioux Uprising or the Minnesota Indian War.

In early August, 1862, attacks were made on white settlers at Belmont, Lake Shetek, the Redwood Agency, Fort Ridgely, and New Ulm. Other attacks took place at Wood Lake in what is now Yellow Medicine County, and in McLeod, Nicollet and Blue Earth counties.

Little Crow joined in the outbreak and became known as the leader. Under Little Crow, the Indians lost the battles of New Ulm, Fort Ridgely and Wood Lake. If it had been the other way around, they might, for a time, have reclaimed their former land and driven the white settlers back to the east side of the Mississippi River. But by September 23, 1862, with the help of government forces, the six weeks' war ended.

There were several causes for the war. Basic to all of them was the fact that just before the white people came to settle in the region, the eastern Dakotas were living there. These Indians were called the Santee Dakotas and were often called simply the Sioux.

Several bands made up this group. There were the wandering Wahpekutes who often visited the shores of Okabena Lake. Others were the Mdewakantons, the Wahpetons, the Sissetons, and the Yanktonais and Yanktons who also came into the region on hunting expeditions. There were about 6,200 in all.

The Dakotas had in the recent past made their homes in the lake and forest area of northern Minnesota, but had been forced south onto the prairies by the Chippewas (Ojibways) who had firearms from the whites they had associated with. Once they lived on the prairies, the Santees depended on bison as did the Plains Indians.

The first group named, the Wahpekutes, were already referred to by early explorers, traders and historians as less than desirable citizens. Some had been outlawed by their own people.

Keep in mind that the Indians thought of the land as their own. It was where they had lived, roamed, hunted, fished. They had been free except for troublesome tribes in other parts. So from 1851 on, when white people began to filter into Minnesota Territory and needed land for farming, there was a threat to the security of the Indians.

Representatives of the federal government and of the Sioux met near what is now St. Peter to work out a deal. The result was called a treaty, an agreement by which the land of the Indians would become the land of the whites. The Indians were to be paid by the government for the land.

Treaties that weren't kept played a large part in the conflict. By the Treaty of 1837, the Mdewakantons ceded to the United States all their lands on the east side of the Mississippi River. Only 14 years later, the Treaty of 1851 forced them to give up their lands on the Mississippi and the Minnesota rivers, in Minnesota Territory. The Treaty of 1858 attempted to break up the community system of the Sioux. They were given homes and work; they were to become farmers and live like white men. But the Indians were displeased with the arrangement and discontented with all the whites coming into "their land."

By that same Treaty of 1858, land that had belonged to the Sioux was cut to one-half the size allotted them by the Treaty of 1851. Six or seven thousand Dakota Indians were expected to live on reserves made up of two narrow strips of land along the Minnesota River above New Ulm. Each strip of land, one on each side of the river, was 10 miles wide and about 70 miles long and extended along the Upper Minnesota River up as far as Big Stone Lake.

Headquarters for the reservations were at two locations. One was the Upper Sioux or Yellow Medicine Agency (below Granite Falls). The other, below the Yellow Medicine River, was at the Redwood or Lower Sioux Agency (near Redwood Falls). On that reservation land, the Dakotas were expected to reorganize their lives and adjust to a new culture — the culture of the whites.

Payments or annuities to be made by the government to the Dakotas to pay them for their land were often late or partly or entirely withheld. The Indians depended on traders for supplies when they could no longer hunt wild game for their food, or buffalo for their hides or skins. One article stated that the Indians had traded furs and hides for blankets and knives, guns, pork, flour and other needs, so they did not owe the traders anything. But some of the traders made long lists of supplies the Indians hadn't even gotten from them. The traders, then, took out what they said was due them from the annuities before paying them out. And sometimes supplies, though available, weren't distributed equally between the farmer Indians and the less-favored hunters.

It was hard for the Indians to stand up for their rights. Very few had learned to speak and understand English, the language of the traders and government agents. And some of the traders who could speak English could not be trusted. So, when the traders took the money that should have gone to the Indians, what could they or their agents do?

In the fall of 1861 the harvest was poor for the farmer Indians. It was hard to get credit at the stores. Then the winter of 1861-1862 was severe. There was enough food at the agencies, but an Indian agent refused to give it to the Indians until the annuity money arrived from Washington. Another problem was one of communication. The two races, in general, could not read or understand each other's language. The Indians came to distrust the white leaders because they did not know what the papers they were to sign said.

One reason the Indians had a hard time finding food the way they had been used to was that much of the wild game they had depended on had been killed by the white hunters or traders or driven away by the terrible noise of the wooden-wheeled and axled ox cart trains or by the whites moving in onto their land. Also, the whites and mixed-bloods were crossing the Indians' land without their permission. Some of the hunters and traders even brought their goods through the Indians' land, over their paths and rivers, and then traded it with others, even their enemies the Chippewas to the north and with mixed bloods.

By Spring of 1862 the Indians felt they had endured enough hardships. They could hope for a better harvest that year, but they heard rumors that annuities promised them might not be paid.

They thought that if the whites had been forced to take up the Indians' ways, the whites would also object. They felt justified in planning war, for if the white men were fighting each other in the Civil War, then they could also fight the white men who kept crowding closer to their reservations and asking for even more of that land.

Among the Dakotas, a soldiers' lodge that had been formed earlier began to make plans. They felt that while many men of the settled areas of the state had gone with the Union army, this might be a good time to take their land back. And after all, Inkpadutah had gotten by without being punished for killing whites at Spirit Lake, Iowa and Springfield (now Jackson), Minnesota in 1857.

Although it has been reported that there were recognized tribes with many friendly Indians who got along with the whites and would not on their own account have attacked, those who were hungry to the point of starvation and were frustrated and angered by their situation began their attack and others joined them in 1862.

A factor that contributed was the absence (for about a year already) of many of the able-bodied young men called to serve their country and defend the Union in the Civil War.

A small band of renegade Indians had been outlawed by their own people earlier for having killed Tasagi, a Wahpekuta chief, and some of his relatives. That band, under a lawless Indian named Inkpaduta, was credited with the killings and destruction in northern Iowa and southern Minnesota in 1857.

The hostilities had already begun in 1846 when a band of

Indians broke up and plundered and drove away a party of government surveyors. Two years later (1848) they attacked more government surveyors. From then on, the few scattered settlements along the Des Moines River were robbed and made victims many times. In 1850 a military post was set up at Fort Dodge in northern Iowa. In 1853 the post was abandoned. The troops went north and established Fort Ridgely on the Minnesota River above New Ulm.

After the soldiers left northern Iowa, the Indians troubled the settlers. When Inkpaduta and his band were refused a share of the annuities, he and his followers returned to their "haunts" on the Big Sioux River. On the way, they learned where the homes of the white settlers were, how many occupied each house or cabin, and what the conditions and surroundings were.

When the people at the older settlement of Smithland, where the Little Sioux flows into the Missouri River, refused to be hospitable to the tribe, Inkpaduta and his men became disagreeable. The settlers ordered the Indians to leave. They did, but they were angry. As they returned over the route by which they had come, they started robbing and destroying the scattered settlements. They were angry enough to kill those who were in their path.

Minnesota was admitted to the Union as a state on May 11, 1858. When the Civil War broke out, Alexander Ramsey was governor of the state. He offered President Lincoln a full regiment of volunteers on April 14, 1861. They were accepted and sent to the front. Other regiments also offered took men from their frontier homes to the battlefront before the first Indian outbreak on August 17, 1862 at Acton in Meeker County.

During the six-week Dakota War, according to the references, about 500 whites (civilians and soldiers) lost their lives. At least 21 Indians were believed dead, though it may have been more. The figure is hard to arrive at because of their ways of taking care of their wounded and dead.

Trials followed. About 300 Indians and persons of mixed blood were sent to be hanged, but President Lincoln ordered a review. The result was that on December 26, 1862, 38 Dakota Indians were hanged at Mankato. Others were taken to a prison camp at Davenport, Iowa. About a thousand dependents of those hanged and imprisoned, along with others who escaped capture, eventually moved to a reservation in southeastern Dakota Territory, on Crow Creek. Others spent the winter near Devil's Lake on the North Dakota plains. Many of their descendants live on reservations in North Dakota and South Dakota.

After the outbreak, the Dakotas not only lost their land, but the payment of annuities was stopped by act of Congress.

As a result of the War of 1862 the trappers, traders, and a few farmers who had already established their homes in some parts of Nobles, Jackson, Murray, and Kandiyohi counties apparently left. In all of southwestern Minnesota, 23 counties were "emptied of their populations as the frontier backed up toward the east." After what had happened, no white men wanted to settle among the Indians still in the area who had escaped removal or had wandered back, supposedly to fish or hunt.

The area was opened for further settlement after the Dakotas were banished from the state. By 1865 and 1866, raids by Indians had nearly stopped and settlers began to filter back in.

It is possible that this group of 35 settlers, squatters, in the story were found and made victims of the attackers, without any record of that happening. Likewise, it is possible that they left the area before the problems started. If that is what happened, where did they go? In hopes of finding that out, actual names of the settlers (as given in the 1860 federal census) have been used in the story. Perhaps a descendant will read the story and come forth with information about what happened to them.

Bibliography

Anderson, Gary Clayton and Alan Woolworth, eds. Through Dakota Eyes. Minnesota Historical Society Press, 1988.

Buck, Daniel. Indian Outbreaks (il.) Minneapolis, Ross and Haines, Inc. , 1965

Carley, Kenneth. The Sioux Uprising of 1862 (1976).

Centennial History of Cottonwood County, Minnesota (1970), p.6.

Federal Census of 1860, Minnesota (microfilmed).

Gilman, Gilman and Stultz. The Red River Trails — Oxcart Routes Between St.Paul and the Selkirk Settlement 1820-1870. Minnesota Historical Society, 1979.

Haberman, Patrick Joseph. A Selected Omnibus Relating to the Early Development of Graham Lakes, Minnesota. Introduction and Chapter 1, Pre-Settlement Years, 1850-1866, pp. 1-6. Mankato, Minnesota, March, 1964.

Hein, Ruth D. Historical columns in Worthington Daily Globe, January 1990 through December 1994. Worthington, Minnesota.

Hudson, Lew. From New Cloth - The Making of Worthington. Worthington, Minnesota: The Calvin-Knuth Unit # 5, American Legion Auxiliary, 1976.

Hudson, Lew. The Wolff Mound. Worthington, Minnesota: Sioux Archaeological Society, February, 1974.

Luehmann, Maxine Kayser. The Sun and the Moon - A History of Murray County. Murray County Board of Commissioners, n.d.

Minnesota in the Civil and Indian Wars (1890).

Rose, Arthur P. An Illustrated History of Jackson County Minnesota. Jackson, Minnesota: Northern History Publishing Company, 1910.

Rose, Arthur P. An Illustrated History of Nobles County Minnesota. Worthington, Minnesota: Northern History Publishing Company, 1908.

Sioux Archaeological Society, Tanner Cabin Dig (concluding report), site of Fury's Island Park in Nobles County, Minnesota, about 1970.

Sons of Norway Song Book ed. by Carl G.O.Hansen and Frederick Wick, for the songs in Chapters 18 and 19.